THE RELIC

CRADLE OF DARKNESS, BOOK TWO

ADDISON CAIN

©2020 by Addison Cain
All rights reserved.

No part of the book may be reproduced or transmitted in any form or by any means, electronic or mechanical, including photocopying, recording, or by any information storage and retrieval system, without permission in writing from the author.

This is a work of fiction. Names, characters, businesses, places, events and incidents are either the products of the author's imagination or used in a fictitious manner. Any resemblance to actual persons, living or dead, or actual events is purely coincidental.

Cover art by Dark City Designs

For Maya and Sharleen.

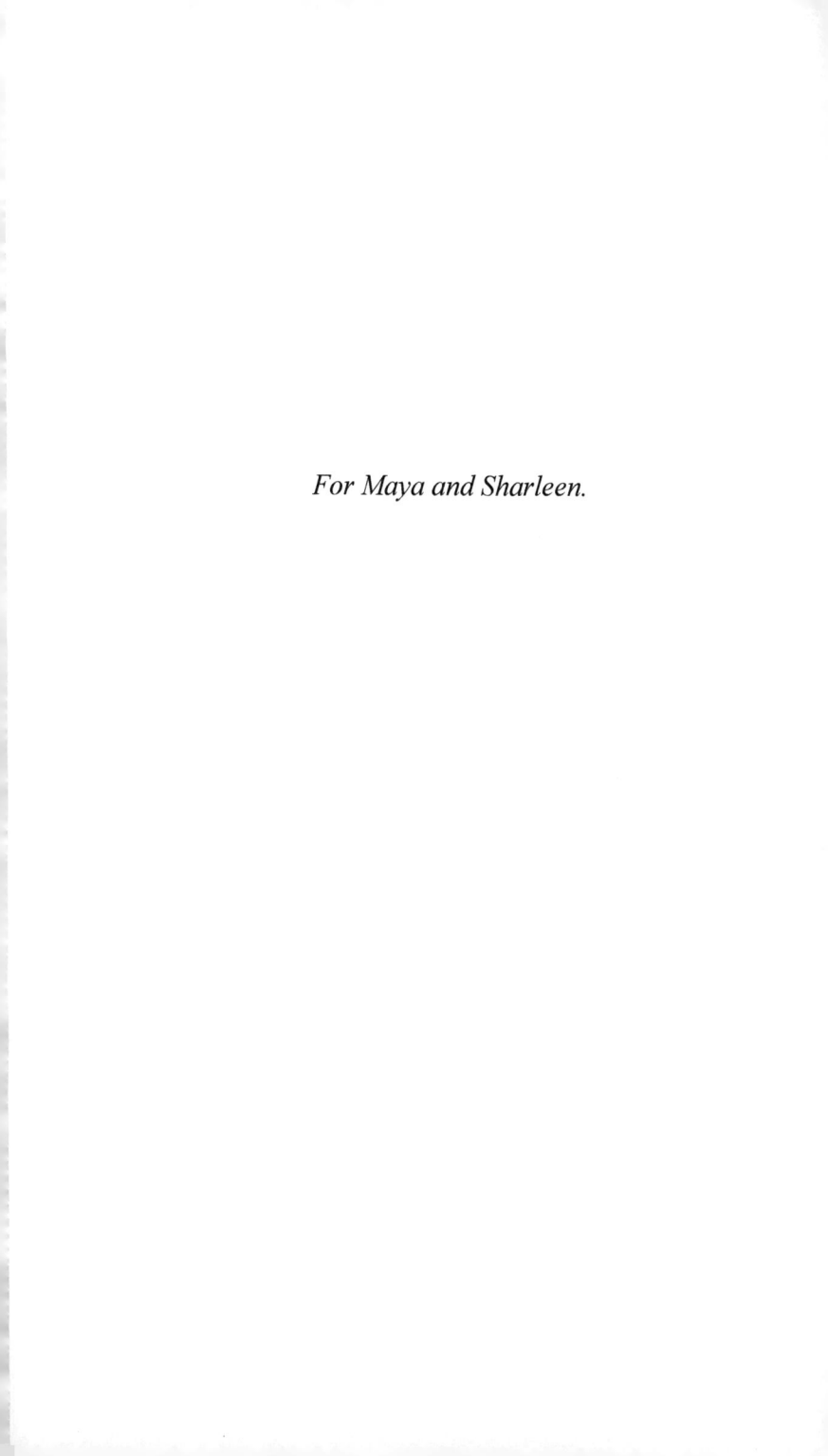

1

VLADISLOV

All thrones, all palaces, all places in this world where creatures of the night lingered—every corner of every continent where hunting grounds might exist—all of it bored me. I couldn't even recall what state the world had been in, the borders of countries, the wars fought, when I last sat as king. Others were placed to carry out that work in my stead. To lord over the night's denizens and keep our kind in line.

Keep my children thriving, learning, adapting, bringing pride to our race.

Darius had been my favorite son, hand-plucked from the Persian court. So much potential... and the ultimate disappointment. Thousands of years were no excuse to forget one's duty and where one came from. Namely from me, who'd chosen him, raised him, taught him, granted him power far beyond what others of our kind possessed.

Power that was abused.

How soon they forget.

So there I sat, on my dismembered son's throne, aghast to be reorganizing a disrupted hive full of Darius' more evil creations. Their minds were... fascinating. Their inability to answer my questions, clever. My son truly believed his gifts set him on equal footing with his creator. Yet all he did was make a mess. What I was seeing was little more than extreme selfishness, even for our kind.

There were secrets buried here, in tunnels that spanned the entirety of this city. Thousands of humans trafficked and kenneled, disposed of with none the wiser.

That, I would give my boy, was clever.

Vampires weren't even a myth in the new world. They were fodder for television shows and movies. Yet thousands lived in this city, hunting, breeding, bickering, and surviving right under the noses of millions of humans.

The evolution of my kind had been curious to observe. From vicious predators who'd ransack entire towns in one moonlit night, to subtle and stealthy, *wiser*, monsters.

Yet, still a bother. Even with all their new rules and new technology and endless opportunities, some just didn't deserve the gifts they were given. And some were not given enough.

Such as my descendent, Jade. Daughter of my dismembered son Darius with so many remarkable talents for our kind, all stripped from her by dear old dad until she was weaker than the lowliest servant. Until her mind was broken, scarred, and required more blood from my veins than—in my long, long history—I had ever given another.

A soft spot I had for my grandchild, though I imagined in ten thousand years, I'd be dismembering her too.

The beautiful imp looked every bit her father's daughter, no denying the resemblance. But only the fates could say what time and power would make of her. Darius was not the first of my creations I'd been forced to *handle*.

He would not be the last.

A flutter. A single unusual heartbeat at that thought.

I'd rather not see Jade fragmented physically. Not after she'd already been so fragmented mentally. I'd see her rise.

Yet now she played house with her strict lover. Now she recovered, her people recovered, the throne recovered, because I sat the throne for the first time since humans traveled over oceans.

Listening to petty squabbles, culling an overripe

herd. Being gracious to my grandchild while simultaneously contemplating war—a mass extinction across all vampire civilizations. The rapture.

Kings and queens all over the world were failing in their rule, chasing pleasure and forgetting to parent. Tithes became poorer, greed on the rise.

Which could be partially blamed on modern times and the infection of selfishness that reigned in all society, human and vampire.

Perhaps a World War was just the thing? Set back this mania, remind all life that death hovered and whispered in their ear.

Without great loss and suffering, what was there to remember to treasure?

Shiny objects? Bitcoin? Art?

The only art I admired these days was the portrait of my granddaughter. Painted myself, and perfect. Life-size, dominating the throne room. A testament of millennia of practice with a brush and the old style of mixing oil paints.

A reminder to the few I had let live of just where their allegiance best rest. The first who had scoffed at it, I ripped in half. Careful that none of their blood might mark the canvas. Purposefully drenching all in the room with bits of dead vampire juice.

Baptized in the blood of a fool. Their one and only warning that she was held in my esteem.

I would have preferred to start fresh with this entire court. Donate some of my own dear flock, augment it with new blood. Find young prodigies with modern tendencies and acumen. But darling Jade had been given the option to choose the fate of this collection of errant idiots. So, I left her a few hundred. Though, to be true, in a year or two, I might return and kill them all if I found myself displeased with how things progressed. Once I deemed her recovery sufficient and forced her to take the throne, that is.

And I would come back. I always came back to this Cathedral, and had every year for near a century. I thought it was my son who drew me, that his inevitable end whispered in my ear. But now he was gone from this place in all the ways that mattered.

Yet still I heard the call.

Which made sitting a throne a bit more bearable.

"My lord."

Ah yes, the one who loved my grandchild. Shining head bowed, manners impeccable, I found I liked Malcom... a very little. "What has she done now?"

These tales were always amusing, his weekly reports while she slept something I looked forward to in this endless slog on the chair.

"She is... perfect." Rushing through his speech

on her recent accomplishments, shaking his head, the man changed topics. Clearly nervous. "I didn't come here to discuss Jade. There is something... I remembered."

It was unlike this one to trip on his words. Which widened my eyes in anticipation and left me leaning forward, fingers steepled, a smirk on my mouth.

"Something"—glowing eyes met mine, concern, a touch of fear as if he might not leave this conversation with the borrowed heart in his chest—"that I must show you."

I smiled broadly, standing from the throne, amused by something different. *Anything* different. "By all means. Lead the way."

∼

Long ago blocked off and forgotten, this area of the Cathedral should not have existed. Not on any schematics, not in the memories of those left alive here or stumbled upon in their excavations. But there it was, hidden behind so many layers of random, unused rooms, barred doors, spiraling ancient stairways so tight one had to bend in half just to navigate the descent.

Any recollection of this place had been ripped as violently as Darius might from every last mind who had ever known of it. There weren't even rats, so tightly it had been sealed. Only damp, and cobwebs, and an utter lack of light.

Even eyes like mine could hardly see in this type of dark.

And I found I loved it. The vibration of the walls, the desolation.

It was a prison, once the burial chambers of the clergy this ground had been stolen from. Cells with iron bars where the dead inside had long ago gone to bone, or desiccated to the point a strong wind would blow them apart like paper.

Other cells had been fully bricked over, whoever was left inside trapped for eternity. And I had a strong suspicion I might've known a few missing vampires of a certain age who, by chance, might grace a cell or two.

And had no interest in relieving them from their box.

Not when I heard something I might only describe as singing, not when I felt drawn forward through that nightmare. Following the siren song, I became impatient of the debris, crushing what I might, tossing it haphazardly behind me for Malcom to dodge.

I moved without his direction straight to a wall

where the bricks didn't match and the mortar was sloppy and thick.

And knocked three times for good measure.

At my back, Malcom confessed, "I put her in here. Ordered the masons to brick it shut... and forgot that very night I'd ever laid eyes on the waif. *Everyone forgot.* This whole area just... disappeared."

Ah. Perhaps dear Malcom was worthy of my granddaughter after all.

As if to soften what he thought to be a disappointing blow, the male muttered, "There is no guarantee she's still inside. He could have taken her anywhere."

Oh, but Darius had not. Not if he'd gone to such trouble to have something so unusual right under my nose. "I can hear her, singing an old tune. Not asleep and not awake."

And ready to be uncovered. Brick... something as inconsequential as brick was all he'd needed to cage a true daywalker. Breaking through the mortar with black extended claws, pulling apart a wall that whined with the removal of each stone, the whole slab having settled and grown accustomed to its missing support, I found a door like any other prison door. Unremarkable and built to make the prisoner know they were there to suffer.

Moments later, that wood was dust, fragments

crumbling with little more than a swipe of my hand. And on the other side? The back of a massive gilded, gaudy, ornate, and hideous mirror. A huge monstrosity of a mirror that completely covered where the door had been.

Tempted to break it, so eager was I to enter, I held back the urge and slid it gently to the side.

To feast my eyes upon a prison cell transformed.

Darius... so predictable. So petty.

To keep this from me! Here.

Underground with the rot. To know what he had wasn't his. To have dared lie about the origin of his child!

He and I would have words about this. Most especially to think that all his golden candelabras and expensive furnishings were good enough for what had been trapped inside. The crypt still stank of blood and sex and tears and longing. Priceless paintings gone to mold in the dank, Persian rug half eaten by fungus and mildew.

Four poster bed, dressed in tatters. Red rags splattered black from old dried blood that still smelled of sunlight, even down here.

Jewels, treasures, secrets.

A room for pleasure derived from pain.

This was a place in which Malcom was entirely unwelcome, and I cast him back before he might set his eyes to the lovely corpse on the bed. "Leave us.

Return to your bride, for her time of rest is almost at an end."

"My lord." Retreating into the dark, he moved with superhuman speed, as if aware how utterly possessive I was of this uncovered treasure. And how tempted I was to kill him just for standing too near.

Pity I had not chosen finer garments for this moment. That I had not brought gifts. My beloved had always loved flowers. Beautiful horses. The scent of pine.

"Here you are, as gorgeous as I remember," I murmured to her withered skull, gently placing my hip to the bed so her remains might not be disturbed. "How long I've waited. Countless centuries searching."

Smoothing back hair that fell from her skull, I leaned over my darling one. "What it means to me to know you kept your promise…" Overfull with a sensation I'd almost completely forgotten, my voice shook. "You swore to me you'd be reborn. And here you are. Sleeping, waiting for me to find you."

Under my nose for a century. Here where she could have been crushed and lost again while I'd let Jade wreak havoc on the building.

My own displeasure was shaking the foundations as it was. Setting a rainfall of dust motes to cloud the room. Leaning over to kiss her mouth—or

The Relic

where her lips would have been had they not shriveled back over her teeth, I tried so very hard to be gentle. "Tell me you knew I'd come?"

The corpse, eyes long ago withered, said nothing. Failed to move. Failed to do anything but lie on a bed stained with her blood. My poor beloved had been alone since Darius had been dismembered, and from the state of the room, alone and suffering. Perhaps I would go into the garden later and have more than a talk with the head on a pike.

Perhaps if the smells under the rot of this place were any sign of what he'd done to her, I'd crush that skull to jelly and eat it.

Blind, my love was blind. Her hearing, the eardrums, I suspected might be intact enough that she at least heard the cadence of my song to her. That she knew I was here, would never allow her from my sight again.

The nubs of her fangs far too short for the work of slicing through my flesh were inconsequential. My true worry was that any attempt to part her jaw might break it, desiccated as it was.

Problem easily solved. I kissed her mouth again then sliced my wrist with a quick flick of a black claw. "Drink and wake. Come back to me."

My blood was poison, laced with nature's contempt for our kind. Yet it contained eternal, monotonous, never-changing life. Pouring it down a throat that could not swallow, I sat with her for the endless hours it took to reinvigorate her, cell by cell.

Nothing was more glorious than seeing my gifts reconstitute lovely blue eyes.

They had been blue in her last life too.

Her daughter's had been that very shade before I changed her into something more. A clue I should have recognized had I paid more attention to the fact that Darius kept my grandchild from my sight.

She took a breath that rattled her half-reformed ribcage. There was pain in those sky-blue eyes.

A flush to cheeks that were fair and high. Dark hair, long and luxurious.

She drank every drop I might squeeze from my veins, swallowed as I gathered her close.

And was so very afraid of me.

That wouldn't do. So, ever the charmer, I spun our tale. Starting at the beginning—this new beginning. "Your name in this life is Pearl. Mine these days is Vladislov. And I have been waiting for you for an eternity."

2

VLADISLOV

Brittle in my arms—half corpse, half goddess—I carried my soul's new form from dust-laden catacombs. As I was in a bit of a mood, any who happened upon me during our jaunt had the unfortunate luck of finding out what they too might one day become should they truly embrace what they were... what human nightmares were born from.

Leathery wings dragged upon the floor at my back, arched over my shoulders, protectively encasing what blindly fought to be free of my care.

It was not just the potency of my blood that had driven her mad. A great deal had been done to my bride. Horrors that were creative—*that might have impressed me*—had they been unleashed on another.

The lack of effort required to see just how

mangled the mind, how traumatized the body, how wrecked the spirit… it was difficult to control my anger.

My gift of blood had left me with a thirst that had not burned the back of my throat in centuries. My veins were bone-dry, and still she was broken.

But I sought no meal. Such irrelevant urges could wait an eternity.

Those curious vampires peeking from their rooms saw what should not exist, and then they saw no more. It took less than a thought to pop their little skulls and leave a mess for another to clean once my path was happened upon. For my darling was too fragile—hundreds if not thousands of years away from learning how to mist through space. More fragile even than the rags on her body flaking away with every writhe as Pearl fought my hold.

She might as well have tried to fight a titan.

There would be explanations and apologies later. I would tend every wound that marked the flesh of her new body, be gentler with her than I had been with any creature since before time. Or at least time by history's reckoning.

Screaming a great deal, despite how I pat. A mewling, toothless kitten, at once pushing the cracked inferno of my flesh and drawing away from the inhuman texture. *Pitch-black* flesh, my eyes a

The Relic

glow of red in my temper, in my elation, in suffering through a mix of emotion I'd forgotten existed.

All I had been over all the ages, all the battles, all the children, all the optimization of a species, had always been *something to fill the time*.

Grief? That, on occasion, teased the outskirts of my thoughts. Dedication? I was nothing if not decided. Boredom? It consumed me utterly.

The world, with all its modern marvels, was really no more exciting today than it had been when my armies swept entire civilizations under my feet. And I suppose, in a way, I was also a touch… probably, yes… *irritated* my love had left me waiting so long.

She'd always been particular. She'd always been beautifully difficult.

Formidable.

Yet I was so beyond in love it stole my breath. So very piqued that rage almost eclipsed joy. The ground shook again under my feet. Sending my children fleeing in the opposite direction of my march.

Seemed not all of Darius' flock was as stupid as they appeared.

Yes, I'd be the first to admit it wasn't princely to lose one's temper in such a fashion. But I wasn't a prince. I was no longer a king. I was a God!

A God who'd found his Goddess trapped in a tomb, withered in mind and body.

Did she just try to bite me again?

What joy! Kissing her crown, I'd never felt more in love.

So cute. Just like the first time she tried to slit my throat all those ages ago.

Our wedding night.

How fond that memory. So fond that I felt the need to cuddle my hissing, screamed-herself-hoarse darling closer.

I might've been old, but I was not senseless to female tendencies. I understood Pearl's terror. It was more than just the current state of my body that brought on this paroxysm. More than my strength, my size, my *altered nature*.

My bride's only interaction with others of our kind had been….

Maybe I would just kill them all. Five or six handpicked old guard would be enough to see to a Goddess' needs. Tens of thousands? Excessive. Yes. That was what I would do. Flock by flock, I'd cull the herd.

Malcolm would have to die for ripping out her fangs. Which would upset Jade.

Who I supposed I had some sentiment for.

There were too many humans these days as well. Easy enough to turn them on one another and let them do the work for me.

The Relic

Hmmm. But nuclear weapons. My bride would not like a sky full of fire and a world full of death.

A Goddess required subjects to rule. Beauty to enjoy.

Revisiting such a thought later would be best. Genocide was such time-consuming work, and no other creature would have a moment of my time save the one screaming memorized Latin prayers from under the membrane of my wing.

Claws, black as the darkest human heart, clicked. Impulsively seeking out the soft thing that continued to beg for the mercy of Jesus. One smell of her divine blood and I checked myself.

Be gentle. Excruciatingly careful.

Taloned feet ceased their march, and I threw back my head in an uncharacteristic roar of frustration, only to realize that my skin was burning her flesh. Powerful wings tightened around my prize as if they might protect her from the very creature obsessed with helping her, and in doing so caused her further pain.

Such irony deserved a laugh.

A madman's cackle that rang out against the stone walls of the vacant throne room.

Fate was such a bitch. Which was why I fucked fate raw and would do so again.

Fate brought me into life mortal. Fate stole my soul. Fate was denied when I tied that soul to me with an unbreakable oath. And fate would be denied again when I conquered my bride's fears and strengthened her body. She who had fucked fate herself by being born half immortal.

Which was endlessly amusing, considering her past.

But the religious babble, those maddening prayers—they were not good for my beloved one. So I offered honest truth, rubbing my chin atop her head, careful not to inadvertently crush her skull. "I met your Jesus. A decent enough fellow, I suppose."

Adjusting my arms to aid in Pearl's comfort, trying to hold a fragile body as cautiously as I might, I added, "Completely wasted the gift of immortality, if you ask me. He spoke and spoke and spoke, and who listened? Who remembered any of it correctly? Not a soul… except maybe myself. Our time in the desert was interesting, though thoroughly misquoted."

Tiny, her reply was. Tiny and meant only for her ears, her lips pressed to my chest as she sobbed. "Blasphemy."

She was so utterly cute that I could not resist running the back of a razor-sharp claw over her cheek. Success achieved, not a single drop of blood spilled. "Oh, sweet one, how I adore you. You're just… delicious."

All fangs and cracked black skin, all flames and searing heat, wings, and bulging muscle... every last molecule of me was completely enamored with my soul's new face. *All of her was delicious*, down to her toes.

I wanted to eat them. Not really. Well, really. But I wouldn't unless she gave me permission.

What had I done to deserve this? This elation!

The loving sigh that billowed, brought tendrils of steam from my lips, was both lengthy and the right amount of dramatic.

In time, she'd look back upon our reunion fondly. And we had time, a universe's endless expansion and contraction of time.

With care, with feeding, with love and attention, my soul would find that it indeed recognized me. That it sang its song so I might be drawn closer.

That deep down she always knew I'd find her and bring her home.

Oh so carefully, I set the shaky thing on her bare, mostly reconstituted feet to spare her skin from further unintentional searing. Perhaps a little too exuberant in the way I slid her down my body as if she might ice the flames. And I was left with a shiver like an untried boy. "Shall we use this moment"—what was the best way to phrase it?—"to outline expectations?"

Blood drunk, healing at a rapid rate, yet still

bearing gnarled corpse's fingertips and reforming organs. Driven utterly mad, for reasons that spread my wingspan and left her cowering, Pearl hid behind her tangled, dark hair.

An improvement. She wasn't trying to run... potentially because I held her slender wrist in my very large, very dangerous fist. And her pretty, filthy skin only smoked a little.

Beating the air with one relaxing flex of my wings, I gave myself the luxury of a deep breath. And contemplated.

She started screaming again.

The bridge of my nose between forefinger and thumb—a habit from my mortal years I'd never quite set free—I even groaned in mirror to her terror, somewhat tempted to let her wrist go. Yet concerned that chasing her through the maze of the Cathedral would only heighten her confusion.

Instead, I tried to explain. "You died in childbirth. Our seventh son." Bitterness welled from a place I had forgotten, lacing a demonic growl into my litany. "Not in some great war, not from a rival's poison... in duty and fealty to your husband." My free hand, tipped with razor-sharp claws, knocked against my breastbone, a loud bang fitting the mood. "The universe dared take you from *me*, and I have squeezed payment from its bones. As you are my soul, there is a chance you

The Relic

spent our time apart in some version of hell you keep referring to." I rolled my eyes toward the heavens, aware of the pun. "If there even is such a realm."

At the widening of her bloodshot, tear-stained, and beautiful eyes, I amended, "Though I greatly doubt you'd have been condemned. My bride is a creature of light. Even in immortality."

Which was, in many ways, hilarious.

More importantly, the creature who suffered through hell had been I. "And now you are reborn and delivered. You are home. With me." Adding, so it could not be said, that despite the form I might bear, I still possessed charm, "And I will love you until time itself ceases to be."

An already fragile mind unraveling before me, my naked, filthy bride screamed, "Satan, has your demon not shown me suffering enough?"

Never having enjoyed that title, I corrected, calm as the precious dead of night, "Call me Vladislov. Or Steven. Do you like the name Steven?"

If Satan got her hackles up, the name she'd known me by in her past life would cause this hissing kitten further distress. Come to think of it, any of the monikers I'd borne over the centuries would. Therefore, Vladislov it would be. Just as she would remain Pearl.

Wouldn't that be nice?

A fresh start that I could improve upon in all ways from our last union.

With a reverence I felt down to my unbreakable bones, I said her new name. "My Pearl." Adding, "And I agree, Steven is too bland. You could just call me 'darling.' 'Sweetheart.' Oh, I'm partial to 'honey.' Bees are such fascinating creatures."

I said it with love—my eyes, though glowing red, my skin, though black, cracked, and fiery, all of it softened with an adoration more eternal than the stars.

In this, she found me hideous and screamed.

How ashamed she was to be naked before her husband.

How brittle her mind after so much damage had been wrought.

And even as she was now, pathetic and weak, I was moved by the very being of her. I always had been a bit obsessive when it came to my soul.

Just as enticing as the original, her form was a song. And though she tried to cover her breasts and pubis, I did look my fill.

I drank her in.

As *she* had drank me so she might live again. As *my* blood fortified her body and would strengthen her beyond measure.

As *my* care would heal her.

This little hiccup of fear… it would be forgotten

once she had more time to learn how wondrous her bridegroom was.

And despite fate's fuckery, one day, Pearl would find me beautiful. For it was not our features that defined what we were, but our shared godhood. And I had spent mine as rationally—as purposefully—as any holy man might. Monitoring legions of vampires while *trying* to leave them free will, an impossible feat I really did not receive enough praise for.

She would appreciate that.

Perhaps that was reason enough not to kill them all? Let them sing my praises and scrape at my feet for her to see.

And once I calmed, fed, and tended to this mess, I would choose a form to please her. One known by vampirekind the world over. One not so beautiful as to stun, but approachable, *real*.

Despite my hold on her wrist, the woman I adored, coveted, and craved above all things fell to her knees before me.

So unlike the queen she had been.

"Queens do not kneel, even to kings." But I wasn't a king. I was a God. And she was not a queen. She was a defanged Daywalker.

Where was my possessive, violent vixen under all this meek ineptitude?

Where was the impulsive, warlike beastie—the mirror of our great father?

Where was the warrior, who the first night I'd taken her to bed had tried to cut my throat? Not that I'd ever faulted her for it. From the day she'd been born, I'd watched her, coveted, peered through the garden walls in which the female offspring of the king were kept, knowing one day I'd be the first man, the only man to have her.

Not even the eunuchs had been allowed to touch, look upon, or pleasure my Jewel.

The Jewel of our kingdom—one of dozens of offspring from hundreds of wives, concubines, slaves, and fodder. But she was the daughter of the Queen. Pure-blooded. A prize no intact male, save our father, was allowed to look upon.

It was even forbidden to me, his favored son. Yet I looked, and I looked often.

She was my soul, and I was her shadow. As she'd breathed softly in sleep, I'd smelled her hair. When she raged against captivity, I'd witnessed her tempers. As she plotted her violence against a fate she did not crave, I'd unraveled her every attempt to be free.

And when I spilled my seed—as was my duty—within the conquered women our empire gathered, it was only her face I saw. Only her body I imagined.

That body that haunted me for millennia.

Her new form, despite the decay and filth, still smelled the same. Like sunshine and the very garden she'd despised. Which had always amused me, as she'd loved flowers, but only so long as they'd been cut, vased, and set out to die.

She smelled like life itself. Uncompromising life.

Troublesome, wondrous princess she'd been.

Dangerous, passionate, wife stolen from me by death.

Pure-blooded sister of a bloodline worshiped by the entire known world.

I'd always admired the incessant and clever attempts to be free of her garden prison before I might claim her and raise her to Queen. That was to be expected, and despite her severe punishments, her every act of insubordination pleased our father greatly. Only a true-hearted Goddess would fight the shackles of luxury for freedom. My docile sisters were left to breed with foreigners and courtiers, their offspring impure. No, only the most determined deserved the role of Queen. Of Goddess.

My Queen. My Goddess.

She dared break her maidenhead on an ivory dagger handle. An attempt to diminish her worth and unravel her destiny.

The knife was delivered to me, blood still drying as a report was made. Though it was long before this world was born, I still remember that first taste of her when I licked it clean. A memory worthy of a smile.

She had dropped the weapon, one that had been stolen from our father—the king of the known world—and smuggled into the harem. Clattering right at the feet of the head eunuch. Blood was said to still be running down her thighs.

And right there, she had lain upon her back, spread her legs, and shown the damage with a grin of triumph... to a guardian forbidden to so much as look, a half-man who could not tear his eyes away.

As if it would not make me love her all the more.

As if I was not to have the eunuch blinded for seeing the precious cunt of my bride.

Naughty vixen. We would have fun with that dagger. I couldn't even recall the amount of times I fucked her with the handle once she'd learned of the physical pleasure she would only ever know under my touch.

That is, once I turned her body into the woman she was born to be.

It was the very reason I left that dagger on her pillow the first night I dragged my new, hissing bride to our chambers.

The first time she had ever left the seclusion and safety of the gardens to learn the truth of men.

The Relic 27

The first time I poured seed into her womb. As our father had poured his seed into our mother. And his before him, and his before him, in a line of kings and queens long forgotten by history—vaguely evoked as old gods by *modern* man, who lived and died long before the pyramids.

They were not gods. I was the only God.

"Please stop looking at me that way." Blushing, her cheeks as rosy as her nipples, she meekly tried and failed to remove her wrist from my grip.

As if I might be capable of turning away from such beauty. Though perhaps the rather large erection pointing her way was a bit insensitive… considering.

I'd never hurt her, but I would transform her. Through tears, gasps, frantic kicking, and ultimate release.

But not today. Not like this.

Not when even after all these years I still remember that… it had taken her some time to love me eons ago.

In that, I was prepared to reevaluate my approach.

These days, I was nothing if not a gentleman.

In my formative years, my father had taught me the ways of our people, of our Queens, of their power and frustrations. How to cow them as a man must a woman, how to physically please in the process, so they might be safe in their furious release and bear strong sons. The strongest sons were always made in battle. Their bodies growing under the changing heart of resentful yet passion-drugged wife.

Until resentment bloomed into respect upon seeing that first bloody baby.

Until it became more than passion shared between a lusty warrior and a strong-willed woman.

Until it became love.

But such was the world long lost.

Such *savageries* were no longer considered romantic or rightful in this time.

I would not rape her.

This time, I would woo instead.

3

PEARL

Three weeks. I knew it had been three weeks, not only by the rise and fall of the sun outside my windows—*windows*, as in more than one—but because something called a digital clock also confirmed the hours and date. Three weeks and I had not left that room, despite the fact that the door was unlocked.

A cozy room, with simple furnishings and warm cream walls.

A room with a feature, a luxury I could hardly describe—a private bathroom.

A private bathroom, where no line for the entire floor collected. Where the warm water never ran out.

Though when I locked myself in the bathing space—who enjoyed such luxuries?—upon leaving, freshly cleaned, covered from neck to toes, I found one wall had been papered. Little flowers, exactly like the paper from my apartment.

Which I now understood had been demolished and something called a mall had been put up in its place.

The exactness of that wallpaper, even the way it was faded and dingy, frightened me.

The exactness of all the things left for me, as if the demon who kept me knew my every secret, was precisely why I knew I was still in hell. This was all a trick of Lucifer.

Even the priest, as he heard my confession, looked at me as if my ravings of demons, of the black abyss, were only a trick of my mind.

I wept when I told him why I was here, that I had killed a man who had followed me home from work and left his body in the snow. That I was damned. His eyes grew sad. "Chadwick Parker died in 1923. That was practically one hundred years ago. What you blame yourself for... it isn't possible."

"You're not listening to me!" And that had to be part of the torment. Those kind eyes so full of pity as I paced and told my story day in and day out. "I've been locked away. There was this book full of entries written in my hand. A box full of notes about demons and hell."

The Relic 31

"You were released from the sanitarium, into the care of your husband and his staff. He loves you, and he's concerned, which is why I was called upon. You're very much alive, and though not many may find Manhattan to be heaven, it is a far cry from hell. At least for most."

Pointing—the glass of my windows bright with morning sun, where people walked in multitudes, where I watched them in utter confusion for days—I cried, "This is not the right world!"

Where were the slender cracked roads and cable cars? Everything from my view was paved and shiny. My eyes took it in with such precision, despite the fact that this room loomed high over the city. Women wore trousers! Men failed to make way for them. Nothing, at least the room that was slowly turning into an odd amalgamation of this new world and my former apartment, smelled like cheap cologne or piss.

"You have the influence to change the world. Wealth beyond measure. The donation made to the diocese will go far to rebuild crumbling churches, extend community outreach. This world is *not right*, I agree. Change it."

"You don't understand what I'm saying…" Because he would not listen. According to him, Vampires weren't real; there was no desecrated church at the heart of the city filled with evil.

And I was falling for kind, brown eyes. The soft tenor of a patient holy man. One who had offered absolution, the Eucharist, the blood of Christ. I was falling for the trickery.

Because *this was hell*.

"Father Patrick, I think it's time for you to leave."

I knew he used the door, as I could see him holding it for *our guest*, but I had been so frustrated, so distracted, that I failed to notice just who had come into my room. Rocking back in my chair, out of it so quickly it toppled, I was at the window, wringing my hands, desperately trying not to look directly at the father of evil.

"Ahh, Vlad. Good morning to you." The older clergyman stood, shuffling toward the door. Pausing to add, "We've read through more of the book of John. She had questions I've yet to address. Considering your theology expertise, perhaps you can enjoy a discussion together on John's finer points."

"Noted." Vladislov gestured toward the door, polite yet brooking no refusal. "Leave."

Not once had the priest questioned such rudeness. It seemed much more than daily prayer could be bought for whatever sum the diocese enjoyed at Vladislov's expense.

Rebuilding churches.

When the door clicked shut and it was just the

The Relic

two of us, he offered a smile. One I could feel, for I still only showed him half my face and tried my best not to look.

He spoke aloud to my private thoughts. "The catholic faiths do love their glitter. I agree the fortune should be spent on the message, not the architecture where limp men try not to ogle the patrons."

Dry lips parting, I dared to defend. "Celibacy keeps the heart close to God."

"But my heart is here." Fingers carded through my hair, the length cut as short as it had been my last night at the Super Club selling cigarettes. Bobbed and angled to land with a sweep at my cheek. A comforting familiar thing in a world of absolute strangeness.

Such as how the man could cross a room so quickly I had not seen him move.

I used to scramble, in those first days when he'd touch me. Cower and cry. I used to feel a heartbeat of pain between my legs, recalling what a demon had done to me in a room Father Patrick had sworn never existed. A room I would understand if only I would keep taking my medication.

Now, I just froze and waited for torment.

In its place, I got a kiss. One on the top of my head. A kiss and a soliloquy. "The book of John was actually written by a woman. When the Christian biblical canon was compiled—the various known gospels sorted through—only four were chosen to tell the message and story that best suited a clear agenda. Her name was stricken, and John was given credit in her place. Isn't that fascinating? The account of the disciple who loved your Jesus the most was written by his wife. Which brings me back to the topic of celibacy. He was not celibate."

I could feel myself splitting down the middle already. "Please."

He took my hand in his, the hand of a man. Veins upon the back, large and warm. Not burning-hot, coal-black inferno.

In place of talons were trimmed nails.

But I knew what he was underneath.

"Would you prefer I came to you that way?" The whisper at my ear was intimate, unwelcome, and sent a shiver down my spine.

Quick to answer, breath left my lips. "No."

"Why won't you look upon me then?"

The father of lies could manipulate his voice in such a way that it stirred me to act. That I felt his longing as if it were honest.

Up went my gaze.

He wore his hair long, in ordered waves any woman would covet. Though handsome, his face was also not. A strange combination of desirable and forgettable. His eyes….

The Relic 35

Hooking a finger under my chin, gently encouraging, he murmured, "There's my daring queen."

I burned, thoroughly, inside and out. Felt it so much deeper than just the flush that ran from my chest to my roots. Those eyes….

"You are safe with me. Safe enough to muster the courage to step outside that door and eat your breakfast at the table… in my presence."

And somehow we were already moving, my sandaled feet walking over the rug, though it felt I left my mind behind me. Still lingering at the window, staring down at a world one hundred years past anything I knew.

Until I was at that window. As if I had always been there.

And Vladislov stood at my door, looking down at his empty hand with an open blend of delight and disappointment playing across his brow. "Utterly remarkable."

Grinning, his attention dragged from his hand straight to where I stood. "Well then, this changes a great deal. So, I apologize in advance."

Before I might shriek or rally, before I could even begin to understand how I had gone from one place to another in the blink of an eye, he bore down on me. A wave of indescribable power that scorched all it touched, stole my air, and then retreated.

Prickles of ice stole over what had been burnt.

What I imagined had been the stink of sulfur teasing my nose with a distinctive crispness.

Pine.

Snow.

Mountains at my feet and a dimming sky overhead setting a distant lake to glitter.

"How?" My breath steamed, a puff that dissipated on a breeze.

"Easy now." Arms came around my middle, steadying a body too cold and too stunned. Warming me with brimstone fire. "Why eat breakfast there, when we can enjoy ourselves here?" Lips came to my ear. "And just so we're clear. If you try to mist away from me, I will follow. Can't have my sweet darling wondering the world all alone. You never know just what might try to gobble you up."

There was a very clear threat in his growl, the beast closer to the surface than the skin of a man he wore to fool the world.

What was there to say when the air was so cold breathing was growing difficult.

To the sound of rending cloth, the size of what stood at my back transformed. Moments later, wings enfolded.

Shivering ceased. A cocoon of vileness tightening as if to deepen the embrace.

"Maya was to serve as your breakfast, followed with some fresh coffee and a scone. She was overjoyed at the opportunity, has feasted upon female virgins for days so her blood would bear a fruity roundness." The beast at my back chuckled. "I know, excessive for a breakfast. I can't imagine what she'll plan should I ever ask her to provide your dinner."

Nuzzling into my neck, the feel of his cracked, searing skin somehow velvet soft with artic air to cool him, he purred, "But I will always be your dinner. And maybe tonight, you'll be brave enough to do more than sip me from a crystal goblet?"

Under those membranous wings, massive hands of fire moved up and down my arms. "Maybe you'll sip from a fingertip, my wrist. When you're truly daring, I'll give you free rein of my throat."

After each private morning mass, a priest told me my ravings were due to a condition. That no sin lay on my soul, that my confessions were delusions soon to be rectified by my faith in God's goodness, mercy, and medication. He left, and *medication* was delivered. Blood. Served on a silver platter in an ornate goblet.

Utterly irresistible, I swallowed it down in great gulps. And felt full, healthy, confused at my inability to fight so deep a craving once my eyes or nose were tickled with what waited on that gleaming platter.

Then I spent my day with a talkative devil in the

guise of a man. Who I tried to ignore, since pleading had gotten me nothing but a lemon cake topped with raspberries covered in black blood.

An odd combination I had practically torn from his hands in my physical inability to refrain.

Thinking of that cake now…

Gums tingling, I felt the part of me that brought the most shame try and fail to lengthen. The thoughts of blood, of blood that didn't come from rats or make me vomit, left my mouth to water.

Laughter moved from the beast into me, more of those stroking hands, my body rigid and famished.

"The cake was brilliant on my part. You've thought of it so often I was concerned it might be some time before I'd be able to impress you so greatly again. But now… my sweet soul has developed a new talent much more quickly than I anticipated, leaving me with endless ideas."

Heaven, help me.

"Would you like to stay, enjoy the view… *with a drizzle of black blood on top*?" He was ever the tempter, and I smelled a drop of blood bloom in that icy air, unsure which part of him had been pricked. But certain I was being toyed with. "Or would you prefer to dine on Marquita, back home, at the table?"

The option of remaining sequestered in my room was not offered.

Yet before I might choose, a thumb dragged over my lips. Chilled cheek cupped in the palm of a monster, I tasted eternity. And opened my mouth for more.

The devil always won in hell. I was learning that daily.

Sucking his fingers because there was no resisting such flavor, his groan weakened my knees.

By the time I was full, sleepy, and drawn into unnatural serenity, I found my legs hooked over his arm, my ear to a chest of cracked pitch. *Cradled.* Like the heroes did in films once the actress swooned.

Warmed by wings that ended in hooked talons so sharp there was no denying they could tear through flesh.

And I began to burn, engulfed in flame for the split second it took for the mountains and ice to vanish and for my room to form around us. There hadn't even been time to scream, and already my skin had mended.

But my clothes were badly scorched. And Vladislov's? His were hanging from his human form in tatters.

"How would you feel about a party?" All smiles, he clapped his hands as if he struck upon the perfect idea. "Tonight! Yes, rest now. I'll handle everything.

And I promise you, no corny shopping montage will be included."

And he poofed away, like a puff of smoke, leaving the scent of pine and firewood.

Falling flat on my rump, I stared at that spot that moments before held the shape of a man, certain I was completely insane… or he was.

4

PEARL

It looked like some movie prop dagger. Curved, the ivory handle etched with figures worn down by ages of handling. Old.

Brandishing the weapon like a dinner knife, a blade gently tapped the goblet of a chilled glass of white wine. Which, considering I'd been told to expect the toast, startled me to the point I twitched.

And then blushed in embarrassment when every pair of eyes in the room darted to and from me so quickly it almost seemed imagined.

The *party's* host, Vladislov, greeted his—or as he continued to remind me, *our*—collected guests with a smile. "Welcome to our little soiree. As each of you has been given explicit instructions addressing the theme of tonight's fun, I will not insult you with a repetition of the rules. Only to say this. If anyone touches or so much as brushes up against my bride, I will end you and your entire bloodline." Jolly, completely unconcerned with the level of violence just threatened, his smile grew. "Are we clear?"

Cheers came as if such an insane declaration only enhanced the drama and pleasure of the handful of vampires in attendance.

"To Pearl!" A man bearing silvered hair and a thin moustache raised his glass—one filled with a far more viscous red liquid.

And cheers arose, my plain name sung as if in praise.

These creatures were as crazy as their king, holding up crystal goblets full of pungent blood. As the only person in the room who ate or drank food, as a Daywalker, what they drank would make me ill. And what I drank was done in private.

Servants in black-tie, tails, each bearing a platter with a single hors d'oeuvre, entered, leaving Vladislov to amend his singular warning with another. "If any of you try to eat any of the special treats for my Pearl, you won't care for those consequences either. They are not for you, no matter how tempted you may be."

How often did this man threaten to kill his friends?

Again, no open animosity on the faces of the

The Relic 43

twenty or so gathered in the apartment's grand room. Only attentiveness as they looked me over, as they lightly chatted and touched one another a great deal. A brush of the arm, a peck on the cheek.

A staged production where every last player was dressed as if they were patrons of the finest club from the 1920s. The ladies: beaded gowns. The gentlemen: starched waistcoats, white bowties, satin lapels in perfectly tailored tuxedos. The music, coming from a source I could not find, was no record. Instead, it was clear as if the singer sat at the empty piano seat across the room to entertain us all.

"Ahh, live music would have been a nice touch. I'm sure someone here has some talent at something." He handed me the stemmed glass of white wine, brushing his fingertips over mine as I took it, *because I needed a drink*. The host, just as spectacularly dressed as the room, eased ever closer. "Olivia, the one in the red dress, dear. She was some kind of performer a decade here or there, though I have no idea if she was even awake during the 1920s."

"The music is fine." This whole charade was already too much.

I was even wearing a dress so exquisite I'd been nervous just to put it on. Nervous of leaving my strange room. Or standing next to Lucifer—

"My name, darling, was never Lucifer. And as much as I am trying not to be insulted, considering the situation, I really…" He paused, rubbed his thin lips together, and chose his next words as if they were foreign on his tongue. "I really *beg* that you think of me as Vladislov. Or anything kinder than comparing me to that prick." For good measure, and while tucking a strand of hair behind my ear, he added—as if infinitely proud of himself, "Please."

And the room was enraptured.

"I, um." I put the glass of wine to my lips and drank, fortified by cool, crisp *nectar of the gods*. "I um, don't know how you…"

How he kept reading my thoughts as if such a thing were natural.

And in my distraction between wine, embarrassment, nerves, and general sense of being completely overwhelmed, I allowed him to grasp my fingers and bring my knuckles to his lips for a kiss.

"I have many talents, as do you. As do my guests this evening. Normal talents you'll navigate beautifully with a little practice." Flicking his fingers, he summoned a servant bearing a beautiful tray with a single treat on top. "Canape?"

"Vladislov." I'm not sure if I had ever spoken his name before.

I couldn't do this. Be here with demons playing dress-up, who I had been told would be dining in their usual style when humans were brought in for sampling later.

The Relic   45

"Deep breath. Drink your wine. Look at me." The orders were effortless. The way he subtly squeezed my fingers, familiar.

Those eyes....

Lifting the snack from the tray, he held it to my lips. "So long as I am with you, my soul, there is nothing ever to fear."

I ate, unsure what a canape was. I ate from the hands of Luci—

"Vladislov." With a wink, he smirked. "We'll work on it."

Acidic tomatoes, something savory I couldn't place. The flavors on my tongue paired with the wine and left gooseflesh on my arms, because a drop or two of the host's blood brought all the culinary glory together. Almost as delicious as the various immortal blood *vintages* I had been served over the weeks.

Probably from the very donors in this room.

"You look lovely, Pearl. The most beautiful woman ever to walk the earth. And I would know," he added with a chuckle. "I've walked it for ages. Never thought I'd be quite so pleased to be robbing the cradle."

Men only gave compliments when they wanted something, most likely to lure a girl into sex.

"As much as I would love to lure you into bed,

that was not my goal in the praise. I love you and simply cannot help myself."

Bed? The last memory I had of a man taking me to bed was so utterly awful the canape was about to come up.

Like a snap of fingers in my mind, what was in one instant horrible and so real I could smell the damp of the cell and feel the burn between my legs, was gone. Just gone.

"Now that, I will stop. I'd rather not fiddle where too much has already been done, but no thoughts of that nature will ruin your party."

The book. The journal. All the entries and explanations of a mind wiped clean each day.

Another mental snap.

"Not tonight, Pearl. All of this can be discussed tomorrow. Tonight, be in the present. Get to know your kind. *Feel safe.*"

And instantly, I did.

Contrition was in his voice, in his countenance. "I apologize. Really, I'd prefer not to, but you require a bit more than handholding to progress into our future."

A servant appeared to pour more perfectly chilled wine in my glass. Wine I drank staring over the rim at my host… Vladislov.

Who smiled an extremely beautiful expression on an interesting face. "Well done, brave queen."

The Relic 47

"She really is a vision." A female interloper. One who approached so regally I felt the need to call her ma'am. And would have had Vladislov not clearly *unh-uh*'d me under his breath.

"Maya, might I introduce my bride? This is Pearl." He kissed my fingertips, met my eyes, and finished, "Pearl, she was meant to be your breakfast."

The statement was so utterly ridiculous that I snorted a quick laugh. Mortified an instant later. Cheeks flaming, I faced the insanely beautiful woman, and said, "Hello."

Insane had to be the perfect word for all of this. All of me. The fact that my hand was still caught in the clutches of the name I would not think.

To which he laughed, full-bellied and thoroughly amused. When glittering eyes left mine, after an improperly long stare, he addressed the patiently waiting woman. "She's shy."

"Weren't we all when life was new? Now come, Pearl, I promised the other ladies I would tempt you from your lover's side so they might meet you."

My fingers were freed, and a hand came to my lower back, propelling me gently toward the woman who countered the space to assure no physical contact was made. Yet still smiled and waved me nearer.

This too made the host chortle, the same host

urging me to follow her. "Go on now. Everyone here will be lovely. Just don't touch any of them." At my back, his voice darkened. "I wouldn't like it. And they wouldn't like what I'd do."

Maya chuckled yet still stepped back, assuring, "He won't always be so obsessive. It's not in our nature to deny physical touch. You'll be hungry for it soon enough. Besides, he'll give you whatever you ask for, including mercy on our poor souls." I followed as she continued. "Besotted, utterly. A fool in love."

Though Vladislov must have heard her, there was no waspish reprimand. Instead, I heard his tenor picking up a conversation about livestock with another, leaving me to the women who crowded as near as they might without the risk of physical touch.

"This is Eloisa, Kami, Fhulendu…" Each lady introduced by dark-skinned, glowing Maya—most of their names beyond my ability to pronounce. Features and hair, histories, body shapes, and style all so foreign, so out of place in the world I knew. Each beautiful to the point it might leave a person breathless.

All patient as I drank more wine and chose silence over conversation with demons. So they spoke to one another for my benefit, of pleasant things, of trysts, of jokes, of modern luxuries I'd never heard of. Of travel and far-off wonders. Of lost wonders. Of their children, their children's children. A few bragging about the pure bloods they had produced, causing others to narrow their gaze as if in envy. Yet all had dozens—if not hundreds of offspring—chosen from the finest quality of humans to enhance Vladislov's vision of Vampirekind.

As if this was normal, they were normal, and the broken piece of this puzzle was me.

I was a Daywalker. I walked in the sunlight, lived with humans, ate their food....

A kiss fell atop my head, a strong arm circling my middle. More tipsy than I realized, I leaned back into the support of something solid when the ground was sand and the world was... strange.

"What a vision the pair of you make!" A round of feminine giggles, then, "I should snap a photo to show my hive. Smile!"

A rectangular device was produced. A flash.

And the ladies laughed, the joke utterly lost on me.

Warm lips at my ear breathed, "Because of the myth that vampires cannot be photographed."

"Oh, like how people think we don't have reflections?" Had I just said we?

I wasn't like these *things*.

Embracing me, another kiss to my hair, Vladislov spoke over the fading laughter. "My bride means no offense. Not that any of you have permission to peek, but her experiences with her kind have been unpleasant. Pearl doesn't know what great company we can be."

"Pearl," Fhulendu, dark-skinned, heavy braid, beautiful to the point I wanted to cry, said, "sometime, I'll tell you about my early years. They too had been unpleasant, so believe me when I say I understand. We all do—well, maybe not those purebloods born to this life. But for many who were changed, especially in the old world, it was a challenging period of our existence."

"Well said." Maya smiled, running a hand down the arm of the woman at her side.

And they seemed so nice I didn't know what to make of it.

They felt real. So real I wished I might see what they looked like under their pretty skins. Were they pitch like Vladislov? Did they crackle with fire? Wings? Claws? Fangs dripping venom?

Did their touch burn?

"Only mine will burn you, my soul."

Shivering from the feel of cool lips brushing my ear, I failed to resist when he took the hand dangling limp at my side, lifting my arm so I might cup the cheek of the creature at my back.

I felt a face freshly shaved, the sharp angles of high cheekbones.

The Relic

I felt my eyes grow wide when he turned his head to press a hot kiss to my palm.

And then I began to cry, because I would not be fooled. Not by Lucifer, or Vladislov, or Darius, bright lights, crystal, beauty that was little more than a husk to conceal real monsters from a world that made no sense.

Breaking down into hiccupping sobs, unreasonably mortified, I was turned, my painted face pressed to the white, starched shirt of my keeper. Ruined by cake mascara and lips painted with rouge.

I sobbed, I clung, and knew I had drank far too much wine too quickly.

My teeth ached; the part of me that had always brought me shame tried to elongate. The part of me, I'd been told, that would not regenerate like any other bit of my horrible body. But would grow back over centuries.

My stomach rumbled obnoxiously loud. I was enfolded, yet there were no bat-like wings. My hair was gathered into a fist, my mouth turned up, and a throat slit with a dagger I knew had an ivory handle poured a fountain of perfection on my face.

I drank.

Climbing the figure who bled in my gaping mouth like a monkey. I burrowed my fingers into bronze waves.

Gulping, rocking my hips despite how my mind screamed to stop such things, agelessness poured down my throat.

When I was done crying, nose stuffed and sniveling, I broke suction on skin that had already mended, smeared in black fluid from nose to breast —rivulets from that once gaping wound having run down my throat, staining the modest collar of the priceless gown.

Looking every bit the horrific vampire.

"Did you see that?" Hushed murmurs so soft no human might hear moved like a breeze through the enrapt room. *"She drank from his throat."*

"She really is his soul."

My hair still fisted in the grip of the man I'd just feasted upon with wild abandon, he made me meet his burning eye as he loudly proclaimed, "And she is perfect."

Before pressing a bloodthirsty kiss to my mouth.

5
PEARL

If one could be devoured, have their very soul sucked from their being, the kiss conquering my mouth accomplished such a feat. I was consumed.

Legs already wrapped around his waist, nails already digging into his scalp so I might hold my prey still while I gorged, I was tangled up with no escape.

Prey became predator.

The tongue twisting about mine was anything but gentle. The palm under my rear had grown claws I knew were black as sin and sharp as the nails driven into Christ.

Yet despite razor-sharp fangs, despite talons, despite ferocity and thirst and monstrous passion, I did not bleed. The demon was careful in his assault.

Hard where I was liquid fire.

Dangerous, snarling, savage, and so strong I never stood a whisper of a chance.

He fed on me as I had fed on him. Uncontrolled. Unabashed.

With a mad mind and unquenched hunger.

Was this how lovers kissed?

Did it always destroy one so completely?

Pain would come next. Rending. Penetration that would kill another part of my tattered soul.

Probably here before the room. Probably over and over until I screamed for mercy while the audience laughed, only to wake up in the crypt to find that book and the horrible notes again.

Yet... as savagely as it had begun, it ended.

The force in which he'd pulled his swollen mouth away left mine searching out missing sensation. An action obstructed by his grip on my hair. "I apologize for being so forward."

What? What nonsense was this?

Men never apologized! They followed women through blizzards and raped them on the street. They locked girls in rooms and caused reckless, horrible harm.

My pupils dilated, the oddest sensation coming over me. Blood drunk and wine saturated, I whispered between pants, "I killed a man when he pushed me down in the snow and tried to shove inside. He might have, I was never sure. But I remember his blood all over my coat. I vomited and scrubbed, but the smell would not go away. So, an angel came to deliver judgment. I was dragged from life into death to be thrown at the feet of the Devil." A living corpse dressed in tatters who poked around every last part of me for a century. "I... I am lost. God no longer loves me."

"The God you speak of never did, Daywalker. Not from the moment your mother birthed you, not from the sad rejection of the screaming child she dumped on the mission doorsteps. Not when you were brutalized. Bewildered. Starved. Or left hanging from that tree as a child."

He took my chin. "*I loved you.* No other."

"You are evil." Of that, I had no doubt.

"Then be my goodness." A peck on kiss-stung lips. "Be my sun."

Yet he could walk in the sun... a thought that left a few startled gasps in a roomful of glittering nightmares.

He could walk in the sun where they could not.

But in that instant, I knew why he burned with fire. He *could* walk in the sun, but he could not feel it. He couldn't feel anything but where my mouth had just been joined with his.

The stroke from buttocks up my spine as he unwound and slid me down his body was a screaming declaration that I was correct. The hands that came to steady me when my shoes hit the parquet floors were black, fire licking from between the cracks in the skin, singeing my dress.

But his face, that forgettable, interesting face, was so human it made my heart ache.

"Let me see." *Show me the night winged demon lurking behind that gaze.*

And he did, to the sound of screams.

Screams that didn't come from my throat.

"They didn't know?" How could those creatures not have? The centuries they'd spoken of. The epochs in which they had known this being.

The room was empty, those who could vanish without a trace gone. Those who could not having fled through the door.

"They didn't know." Fanged and hideous, a monstrosity smiled, preening, wingspan stretching to knock items from carefully arranged tables and crash against crystal chandeliers. Making a right mess. "Only you have seen what becomes of a man whose soul is stolen. Who will make any sacrifice to see it returned. Who has been trapped in endless monotony waiting for his lost love to be reborn as she swore she would be."

But others had seen him when I'd been pulled from the tomb.

Chuckling, running strands of my dark hair

The Relic

through his claws, Vladislov said, "Not any who lived."

My next words died on my tongue, what he'd implied sinking deep into my belly. "So, you're going to kill all of your friends who came tonight?"

His response was so simple. "Yes."

"And if I asked you not to?"

"Not to slaughter the monsters you feared?" A shrug. More crystal shattered against the floor when those terrible wings flexed and bent. "I suppose I could restrain myself. But… it's going to cost you for the terrible mess your request will create."

Of course. The devil and his deals.

"Ah, ah." That thing clucked its tongue, bending over me so I need not crane my head so high. "There is no need to always think the worst of me. I can't help but love you, and I am trying rather hard. Be kind."

Kind?

Maya had let it slip in might conversation that I held their lives in my hands. Had they been as terrified as I to be there?

"Some of them, yes." The beast slouched and took a knee. Like a knight—like a villain. "It seemed only fair you not be the only frightened person in the room. Please note how I called them *people*. Your train of thought tends to be a bit less gracious. And mayhap you'll consider that none of us had a choice in what we became. Not really. Not when the orchestrations of the universe are so… unavoidable."

Braced, knowing exactly what men wanted in trade, my fists bunched in my skirt.

This creature was very male. I had already seen what the tatters of his clothing could not conceal on more than one occasion. An organ massive, inhuman, and pulsating.

Yet, as I was already condemned, already made the whore in that god-forsaken pit. What did it matter if I did this for strangers? "Do you want me to lay down here?"

A great sigh sent heat to ripple in the air, Vladislov answering, "I want you to go for nightly walks with me, *outside*. Once every three nights, we'll take dinner in a restaurant. Where you can order anything you want and I can spoil you with compliments."

Why such a simple thing seemed more terrifying than spreading my thighs, I couldn't say. A cold sweat on my brow, dryness on my tongue, I nodded. Because there was no agreement to be made that wasn't even more ridiculous than this party.

"Well, that settles that. They can live. They will adore you for such mercy, clever queen!" How it smiled with that face, I couldn't comprehend. Not that I wanted to, or even stood a chance.

And just like that, he was gone. One moment there, the next not.

I was alone, in a roomful of broken things and scattered glasses. Of immortal blood spilt on the floor and smeared into my skin. What was there to do but seek out the trays of food that had been dropped by the staff and snack? What was there to do but walk over all that shattered crystal and feel my dress catch on the shards?

What was there to do but drink every bottle of wine left to chill until I was thoroughly intoxicated.

Passed out sprawled across a settee.

To hardly wake when strong arms lifted me up and put me to bed.

Cool sheets below, the mattress dipped and a warm body joined me.

And I slept like the dead.

6

VLADISLOV

"Ha! I knew this experience would be something. Just look at your face." She was adorable with her eyes squinted and her cheeks sucked in. "I used the Yelp."

Mouth still full of overcooked oyster, my soul asked, "Yelp? Like a howl?"

As if this were some new Vampire power she'd yet to see. How hard it was to restrain the laughter, but I did.

Heroic as ever, I brandished my smart phone and pulled up the app so she might see. "Newspaper editorials are a thing of the past. Now, anyone can blab an opinion for the world to see. As humans so love to complain—especially where they think they might be heard the loudest—a clever monkey designed a platform where people might review a business and then all glory in their opinions."

Baffled, she stared down at the platter. "So humans like this dish?"

"No. They hated it. And now you are part of that experience! Welcome to the twenty-first century." Passing her my phone, a device it had taken three days to convince her to touch in the first place, I grinned. "Want to leave a review?"

Missing the concept, but so cute I could literally eat her, Pearl leaned closer to my outstretched hand and told the phone. "The seafood platter isn't good."

"Ah." We'd work on how to use the keyboard later. Tucking my phone away, I pushed back the wobbly chair, in full agreement with how it groaned over uneven wood floors, and offered my queen a hand. "Now, let's see if humans are correct about the bistro next door."

Sipping water, still somewhat grimacing, she gave me such a pathetic look. "Does the Yelp say the food there is also bad?"

"No. The chef is a hidden treasure, and she has prepared a feast specially tailored to your tastes tonight." Which I had assured by sending Fhulendu with her favorite human pet to scout out the location. The human sampled every last dish on the menu, required to fully report each sensation. A twenty-five-page essay waiting for me to indulge in, mostly glorifying the merits of the braised lamb shank. "If you like it, I'll buy the location. If you're extremely happy, I'll kidnap the chef and have her changed. She can prepare your meals for eternity!"

Considering freshly changed humans were such a massive pain, the generous offer most assuredly would impress her.

Except it didn't.

Though I knew Pearl required sustenance of the mortal variety, the snip dared lie to me, placing her napkin on the table. "I'm full. Thank you though."

This wouldn't do. "Someday, you'll see a human *you just have to have*. You'll know your offspring at first glance, or maybe first smell. We, like any species, reproduce."

"I won't turn a human into"—she gestured at herself, so full of self-loathing it made the air taste rancid—"this."

"No. You won't. Daywalkers can't. I will have it done for you." This lesson was far more imperative than the Yelp, honestly. Or even her discomfort when I pinched her chin and raised her eyes to mine. "Mark my words. It is natural and normal. As is reproduction of the more erotic variety. We are a very physical species."

What power a bit of fresh air and bad food had on my darling. She brushed off my hand and even had the tenacity to glare as she sneered. "I don't want children of any kind."

"Your daughter might be hurt to hear you say so."

Check and mate.

Color draining from her cheeks, Pearl bit her ripe lip. Tugging it between her teeth in a gesture so disconcerted, so dumbfounded, that when her eyes went side to side as if taking in the room—as if the truth might be found on the sticky floors or on the mismatched furnishings—I twisted the dagger, so to speak.

"Her name is Jade. She has... had... your eyes and the temperament of a lonely kitten. I like her quite a bit." Tucking Pearl's arm through mine, I pulled her resistant self from the restaurant. "She has your gift of sunlight. Appreciates fine cuisine. One day—when you are ready—a dinner would suit."

"I have a little girl?"

"She's in her seventies. Woefully neglected by her now decapitated father. Bitter, and absolutely in love with a warrior named Malcom. They are to be married soon. I expect a pureblood child will follow shortly after. Daywalkers are extraordinarily fertile."

"I have a child who's the same age as I was when—"

"When Malcom—the one you described as an

angel—ripped out your fangs and brought you before Darius for crimes unknowingly committed."

Shame, horror, there was even a catch in her voice. "She must hate me."

"Oh yes, she does. But she also doesn't know you exist. We all assumed her mother was a human Darius made a meal of. Even I, her grandfather." Bloodlines were complicated, but my next statement was plain as night and proffered with a charming wink. "Or should I say stepfather, now that we are one? Either way, she's a proper combination of our lineage and will therefore be on equal footing with all our fat-cheeked future babies."

Before us, the door of the bistro opened, one of the multitude of servants who prepared this corner of the city for our walk playing their part admirably—assuring everything was as smooth as the dark, silken hair of my bride.

I deserved a medal!

Maybe a kiss.

Instead, and it was so unexpected that despite her miniscule strength, Pearl threw off my arm. She threw it off, shook herself as if to remove something disgusting, and turned on the sidewalk I had scrubbed clean only the night before.

And she stomped away.

"Darling, the food will get cold!" She wasn't listening, prancing off as if I might actually allow her out of my sight. Trotting after her, I tried to smooth extremely ruffled feathers by calling out, "Come now. How could you think such things of your own children? Of course they won't have batwings. You're not spawning imps!"

Tearing at her hair, my soul screamed, "Stay away from me!"

This would not do. Nor would my budding temper serve. Unfortunately, a note of the demonic snarled through my voice. "*We had an agreement.*"

Hackles up, she spun. "For a walk and a dinner. I walked, and I ate whatever that foul thing was."

"An oyster, breaded, and coated in mayonnaise. Worst in the city, according to the Yelp."

Her little filaments of rationality were snapping. I could hear it her thoughts were so loud. Not only that, she was actually angry. Not scared or horrified. *Pissed off*, as the youth liked to say.

So angry she dared point a finger and yell. "You are absolutely insane!"

Pot meet kettle.

Yes, I rolled my eyes, somewhat giddy that we were having our first lover's quarrel.

"Did you just—"

Smoothing my navy dinner jacket, I adjusted the cuff, inspecting the tailoring. "Yes, I did. I rolled my eyes at you, because you are acting like the baby you imagine flying around and snatching up tourists.

My feelings are getting hurt. I do have those, you know. Just as I have infinite patience and will follow you, *humming a jaunty tune*, no matter how far you walk. And, yes, I know you walked from California to New York City. I know everything about you, Pearl, in this life and your last. Why not try to get to know me? Have I been so terrible?"

Guilt… there it was. The weakness of all good souls. And my soul was pristine. Pristine with high color and a trembling lip. Regretting yelling at Satan himself, how cute.

Tucking her hair behind an ear, she muttered, "What am I to do with you?"

"Tolerate me." Smile back in place, I strode closer and offered my arm. "Eventually, I'll grow on you. You didn't love me at first when I took you for wife in your last life either."

"Why not?"

A valid question I would never fully answer. "It was a different time, and you didn't want to be Queen. Unlike this incarnation, you had lived a life of pleasure. Like this life, you had been denied fulfilment. Back then, I swore to you you'd find it in our children, just as our mother had—"

Aghast, she tripped on an uneven bit of pavement. "Did you say *our* mother?"

I'd have the sidewalks repaved to be even in this part of the city. No stubbed toes for my bride. "As I said, it was a different time. Earlier than even the Egyptian pharaohs western culture so obsesses over. So ancient that everything about our people was absorbed into new people. Into budding cultures, kingdoms, *religions*. But I digress...."

And she'd had enough. "I've never had a gentleman caller, but from couples I'd observed at the Super Club, umm..." Toying with her fingertips as she mustered the courage to explain whatever this was, Pearl took a deep breath. "These would not be considered appropriate topics for courtship. Especially unchaperoned courtship."

Canting my head to the side, I puckered my lips, considering. Then I stole a peek—a little one. The fantasy sweet Pearl had daydreamed was of a man who wanted to talk to her, to introduce her to his parents, who didn't care that she was half-starved, disgusting, and poor. Where she could pretend she was human and wouldn't have to watch him slowly age and die.

How sad to have lived a life never knowing she had a whole family waiting for her. A family who would never age. Who would love her.

Uncharacteristically pensive, I murmured, "I see that I was right."

It would be that first baby that would make her love me. A beautiful, perfect cherub that would nurse at her breast and drink of my flock.

But this I could not say, because it would just *stir the pot*. Pearl was already half-mad, and it would be centuries before that damage might mend.

Fuck you very much, Darius.

Oh, was I going to have another long talk with my son. The nightmares I would inflict on his mind. And I knew exactly what his next torment would be. Poetic justice.

I would make him relive every single night Pearl suffered in the crypt as if he were she. The perfect sentence. One I could carry out over and over and over until the sun ate this planet and my people repopulated a new one.

Tapping her foot in a feminine gesture passed down through the ages, I came back to the present to see Pearl's arms crossed under her breasts. Her lovely lips turned down.

"I was right." I amended, "In saying I'd follow where you walked. But I was wrong on other counts. Screw the Yelp. I should have asked you where you'd like to be treated on our first date."

That threw her for quite a loop. Shoulders relaxing, my darling one lowered her arms. "I don't even know what street we're on, what year it is, or what I would have liked."

"Quite right. Furthermore, no more talk of Jade, or *ancient history*. It was uncouth to assume you'd be thrilled about children as if you'd waited an eternity as I had." I was salvaging this beautifully, despite the way she unconsciously clawed at her forearm.

So beautifully, in fact, that she said, "Well... we shouldn't let the food get cold."

Offering my hand like a proper gentleman, I said, "Despite my failure to ask, which I won't repeat, I do think you'll be pleased. The Yelp is a hilarious mishmash of human snark and assholery. But, it has its uses. If you like, I'll teach you how it works so you might live dangerously and pick where we eat next."

"I want to try fast food. Like from the commercials." What a lovely glow came to her eyes before she announced, "Tacos!"

My love was completely insane, but even I was aware of humans' delight and the necessity of tacos. "Done. And then I will introduce you to something so popular I don't even know how to describe the human reaction to it. A taco truck."

Our dinner was lovely. Pearl drank wine and ate her fill. So content that she let me feed her from a vein when we returned to our temporary home. Albeit the vein was in my wrist. And, unfortunately, she closed the door to her room on me when I tried to follow her in.

I was only going to hold her, and maybe steal a kiss.

Between her legs….

So instead, like a mongrel without a world begging to fuck him, I took my member in hand and stroked out a release. My thoughts full of Pearl, listening in on her dreams and lightly inserting the arousal I felt as my seed sprayed my chest.

Her mind responded in kind. In sleep, she orgasmed.

7

PEARL

Back bowed, I woke to a symphony of sensation that left my gasp punctuated with a shameless cry. Pulsating from my pelvis, another wave of feeling broke. Leaving my mouth gaping on another relentless, unstoppable moan.

Sweaty, panting as the dream faded and reality stole in, I sat up. Staring down where my nethers were covered by sleeping gown and blankets. Completely confounded.

What on earth?

"I heard a cry! Are you okay?"

Clutching the sheets to my breast, my head shot up to find Vladislov shirtless, wearing drawstring pajama bottoms, wiping his chest with a towel. One he then dropped on the floor as if it had never been in his hand. All the while stepping closer to my bed.

And still, I tingled, turning my eyes from his half-nakedness and trying to piece together some semblance of an answer. Because what could I have said?

Mortified, unnaturally hot, all I wanted was to fan my face or hide under the covers. But I had cried out rather loudly, and of course someone would have heard.

"A dream." Not that I could remember it now, or even recall my name in that moment. "I'm fine. Sorry if I worried you."

The bed dipped, and a male wearing *no shirt* sat next to me. He did this despite my discomposure, even resting a hand on my blanketed knee.

Leaning closer as I stiffened, shivered, and blushed, he said, "You look rather flushed, Pearl. Do you need anything? Water? A cuddle?"

My nipples were hard, poking against the simple cotton of my nightgown, covered by the sheets I clutched to my breast. And my breasts themselves... ached.

Water would be perfect. An entire frigid bath of it.

Instead, I was given heat. Heat in the voice of velvet offering solace. "You're shivering, Pearl. Shall I warm you up?"

Before I might think of something coherent that might drive him off, my bare arm was stroked, a wake of pure fire left where I had been touched.

And it burned so beautifully in places it should not that I groaned in frustration.

"This won't do, my dear." Gathering me to him, Vladislov somehow already under the covers, I was pulled to that naked chest. "Let me hold you."

Finally, my tongue unhinged. "You're not dressed!"

Words waving off my valid complaint, he embraced me all the tighter. "In this era, men do not sleep with an upper covering. I like to keep my costume fitting with the times. Wait until you meet Vampires who still wear powdered wigs or mud for clothes. Ridiculous."

There was a heart beating under my ear. There was warmth further invading the thin cotton of my nightclothes. The smell of smoke, spice, a cedar forest at night.

The body of a man intimately touching me in a way that wasn't carnal but extremely intimate. Even tangling his legs with mine.

A man so strong I wouldn't be able to stop him when—

"I didn't come in here to have sex with you, Pearl." That big, warm hand moved up and down my spine. "You cried out, and you need comfort."

Which sounded reasonable.

But half-naked? Touching me? Another, last, impossible series of twitches left the place between my legs clenching at emptiness, when his leg shifted just so.

Gulping air, I succumbed to the tail end of a shiver and... finally, mercifully... whatever had possessed me abated.

My wits returned, and though I appreciated that the flaming blush of my cheek was hidden, tucked as I was under Vladislov's chin, the entirety of this situation was wholly improper.

Shushing me, rocking my body as one might comfort a child, he said, "It's late. The sun is going to be up soon. Close your pretty blue eyes. I'll be here, always."

Arms somewhat awkwardly caught between us, I debated on trying to move. Unsure how to accomplish the feat without touching hard muscle. How to position my head so the hair on his chest would not tickle my lips.

"You're still shivering. Here." Out of the darkness, a membranous weight landed over my body. A wing attached to a very human body. One Vladislov tucked around us as if to shield out the rising sun, the world.

Leaving the pair of us in a vacuum.

The only two creatures wrapped in night.

The Relic

Twisted together in limbs, in flesh. Opposing forces completely and utterly intermeshed.

To the music of his heartbeat and my breath.

"This isn't seemly." My complaint was half-hearted, as such heat made me drowsy.

Self-satisfied, a grin in his voice, he replied, "What could be more natural?"

Is that what married couples did? Did they embrace this way?

No creature had ever held me in such a fashion. Not that I could remember... though the journal had mentioned nights I had been happy in my cell.

So this had to be a trick by the infamous trickster kissing my crown and mumbling to me in some unknown language.

"It takes *practice* to learn the role of wife. To be plucked from the garden and placed in the bed of a king. To discover the power you wield. How at the crook of your finger I would topple worlds. How at a kiss from my lips you'll know pleasures that will make my name sing from your spirit."

One man's pleasures had forced blasphemy from my mouth.

"I would never hurt you that way. What Darius did to you was a perversion of coupling. Your experiences prior to the crypt were against your will. You have never been made love to, and have good reasons for your fear."

In that winged cocoon, in the infinite intimacy of the moment, I grew angry.

Not just about the things that had happened to me over the entity of my pathetic life. But about what I had seen in the weeks since I'd come out of the dark. Couples walking hand in hand on the street. Kind glances and loving strokes. Laughter.

The films I'd been shown on that strange flat screen with their adventure and happy endings. Respect and jokes and fun.

I was never going to know those things.

How he did it—perhaps he grew a third arm—but suddenly my awkward arm was gathered, fingers trailing to mine, where they interlocked. "But you're knowing them now."

"You say that as if this is real," I confessed. "But I'll wake up back in that tomb."

"Even if you should, it's just a room. And there is no room on this entire planet that could hold you should you wish to leave it now. I can teach you why you never need to be afraid of that room. How you can move through space with a thought—to anywhere you desire. Or always to me, where my arms will be open. Where you will never feel pain."

Bitter and suddenly sad, I muttered, "Is that how you tempted Jesus in the desert?"

"Tempted?" Dry laughter filled our secluded space, shook the chest under my ear. "I've never understood how the various versions of that story all got it so wrong. If you want to know what happened for those forty days and forty nights, you're going to have to ask Jesus himself. Though his name is pronounced *Yeshua*."

"What you are saying is sacrilegious. Jesus ascended from his tomb to return to his father."

"He walked out of that tomb after the stone barring him in had been removed. And he's a stuffy, cantankerous bore. Constantly whining about the ways of the world yet refusing to appear and explain himself." With a derisive snort, Vladislov added, "The second coming. What a joke.

"And let's not forget the other figures before him, just as determined to educate the cattle. Mani, Krishna, Romulus, Glycon, Zoroaster, Buddha, Heracles… need I go on?"

The term cattle was not one I enjoyed. Reminding the nightmare wrapped around me, I said, "I'm half human. And I drink from you. Does that make you cattle?"

The beast dared reach down and give my rear a quick grasp, chuckling. "I would gladly be your bull."

Unable to shake off the fingers entwined with mine, I couldn't give him the swat he deserved. "That is not what I meant."

"But you wouldn't blush if I didn't tease. And I adore the way you blush."

Wriggling to get away only got me more encumbered. "Are you an octopus? Where did all these arms come from?"

"Can't a man give his wife an extra hand or two?"

He was impossible. "For the love of all that is holy. Can you be serious for five seconds?"

"I am the embodiment of seriousness." Lips brushed over mine the instant he spoke those words. Which was impossible, as I was still resting on his chest and nowhere near that mouth. "Drab as he is, Yeshua, is the only person, outside of myself, who can tell you of our time in the desert. Since we both know you won't believe a word out of my mouth, I'll arrange for you to spend time together. Though sometimes it's better to hold on to our delusions than face the truth of the world. Consider that should you really want to speak with him."

"Jesus is in heaven!" My snarl earned me another phantom peck.

"Many people do consider Brazil heaven."

"I will not lose my faith." By God, I would not.

"Your faith?" Playfulness drained from the monster, fingers that had been tickling ceased movement. Form curling even more around me, like a centipede eating a bug, razor-sharp fangs found my throat. Scraping *oh so softly* over that tender place. They dragged from neck to my earlobe. Where he nipped, yet drew no blood. Where he whispered, "Your faith, you say? Was it your choice to be abandoned on the doorstep of a mission? Did you have a say in the education those monks graced you with? The beatings, the labor, the abuses of a particular priest? Did they not tell you to fear God and obey? Did they not take advantage of a dependent child with nowhere to go in a world that was savage and dirty, crawling with prospectors looking for gold? At no time was it *your faith*. It was and is your shackles, imposed upon you by a world that use religion as means of control. And if there is this God you imagine, she would agree with me."

"God is *not* a woman." Women were creatures born of sin. The reason humanity fell from grace.

Wing lifting, all touch retreated. Brightness broke through our private circle, causing me to squint at the unwelcome intrusion. Leaving me with the face of a man who looked disturbed, a bit angry, and even sad.

A man with his outstretched wing folding at his back as if he were an angel, even though the wing was that of a creature from the pit. One propped up on an elbow, watching me in silence, bathed in sunlight.

Minutes passed, with each tick of the clock my

shame growing, though I was unsure what sin I had committed. Endless hanging silence that left me fidgeting and unable to hold his gaze.

Unable to beat it another second, I muttered, "God cannot be a woman."

"And the world cannot be round. And humans cannot land on the moon. And evolution is not factually based because the most popular creation myth of this era had everything burst into life in seven days. But you don't know that word, because you were raised as a practical slave under starvation conditions. It took you decades to learn how to write, picking up snatches here and there while you wandered from city to city. Famished for education, but female, weak, poor, and frightened. There is nothing evil about you. But there is evil in ignorance. Ask me how many verses of that bible I could quote to support my argument?" He reared back, haughty and grim. "Actually don't. I have no interest in wasting my breath. You can't hear, because you are broken. And I am gravely insulted by all you have said."

Why was I crying? Why were hot tears falling down flushed cheeks? "But you don't understand. God cannot be a woman. He filled Mary with child."

"The immaculate conception? Winged angels in the sky at the birth of Christ?" Unfolding the wings at his back, Vladislov beat them against the air, raising himself from the bed as if to take flight. "Gift from kings who'd traveled far. Gold, frankincense, myrrh. All priceless items left at the feet of a peasant woman and her swaddled baby."

My mouth opened, but I was cut off by another beating of his wings and a louder riposte. "Just to make it clear in case you are not picking up on the subtle hints I've layered through this chat. Mary enjoyed my cock when we lay together. For birthing my offspring, she was rewarded with riches. And to many, I am a God. But the only God I worship has a cunny. And I know this, because I have seen you gloriously naked. Wordplay or no, I will not have you insult my Goddess, my love, or my tireless devotion. You will be educated, starting tonight. And you will meet with Yeshua in time and find yourself in a world so far beyond what you allow your mind to comprehend that you will hate me for it."

Crying all the harder, I put my head to my knees. This only angered the pacing tiger, who grabbed something and threw it to shatter against a far wall.

On a roar, he demanded, "Tell me how to make this stop!"

And I snapped. "Just hurt me already! I'm worn sick from waiting!"

Lifting up an entire chifforobe in rage, Vladislov

ripped it apart. No longer man in form, no longer rational. He broke the simple things in that creepy room, bellowing smoke and braying like a wolf.

"Hear me, woman!" Demonic in person, in voice, on every level, that winged monster turned on me. "I will not. You don't need a devil. You torment yourself enough to put the entirety of hell out of a job."

8

PEARL

What a mess…

Not just the room, but my insides. Guilt I could not explain weighed on me. More than that, the things he said, about how long it had taken me to learn how to read. How I had drawn letters on brick with rocks. The decades of practice so I might have *one* redeeming quality.

I too could quote scripture… verbatim.

Misspeak and receive a strike with a cane across the shoulders.

As a child, I'd memorized every part of the bible that made it clear to be female was to be evil. I could recite prayer with a rosary until my fingers bled.

I could kneel on rice, be beaten with a stick, and be hung from a tree.

I could be raped.

But I could not navigate this world. Not that I had ever navigated my own well. Always hungry. Always ashamed. Always last in line and first under fire.

Stick-thin, starving, lonely, waiting to be delivered.

Waiting for exactly what now sat before me in ruins. A room with a window. Companionship.

Food.

As embarrassing as it was to admit to myself, I was tired of starving. Rats, stray dogs, bugs when I was especially desperate. Vomiting after a meal. Hearing the priests screaming the first time my fangs elongated.

I had prayed for my entire life to be cleansed of my urges. I felt less.

Because there was a whole world of things so beyond my scope that I just stuttered and drooled like the idiot I was.

A demon had torn every last bit of furniture in my room to shreds. All save myself and the bed. I bore no scratch or bruise.

That was a lie.

My pride was heavily bruised.

I worked hard. I loved to work hard. It was the

only thing I'd ever been appreciated for. Never late, did the job without complaint. The model cigarette girl, or waitress, or cleaning lady.

The very priest that came to offer me the Eucharist each day believed I was mad. I certainly felt it. But I could not forget the feeling of that weighted paper between my fingers, the script in my own hand. Penmanship I had copied from a discarded letter I had found in the streets.

Penmanship of a lady of worth.

Why did all the things in this house always get broken?

Powdered wigs and mud, he said. Yet my costume was from my last years I could remember. Even the nightgown with its ruffled collar and plain cotton. I was the very joke he'd made. Cloche hats, sack dresses, a party in theme to the Roaring '20s.

Ridiculous in every way.

Cold now that the inferno had left. After he had broken sad copies of my former cheap furniture.

The whole room was so at odds with the rest of this *penthouse*. And yes, that was the proper word, as I had been corrected like the idiot I was, more than once.

A veritable castle in a city I remembered but didn't know.

"Cigarette?" My calling card, my trade. A word that came easily to my lips.

A thing that was out of fashion and deadly, not that anyone knew such things back then.

Tobacco caused cancer. Which I would never have. Just like I would never age, and even starvation had not killed me. I was *this* forever.

On a planet that was round.

And apparently humans had walked on the moon. THE MOON!

Staring at the wrinkled cotton of my nightgown, at exposed arms that were no longer barely bone and flesh... I didn't know myself.

And I should have.

All I could think of for those three days I had hung from a tree as a child was how I was born of evil and deserved to die. But never did. The branch broke before I did.

Darius raped me in body and mind, in so many ways I knew I could not remember. And I endured.

Stupid, ignorant, a pointless decoration in the room.

"Please forgive me." Out of nowhere, he arrived, on his knees, his head in my lap as he sobbed. Those wings of his twitching with each massive inhale that stretched his ribs.

Who asks the forgiveness of an idiot?

And what idiot rests their hands on the shoulder of a weeping devil?

I wasn't afraid of the truth, even if I didn't care

for it, admitting, "I am as stupid as you say. I always have been. Stupid and sickly and starving."

Those eyes turned up, cracked black cheeks sparking with flame turning his tears to steam. "I was wrong… and foolish. As much as I hate your evil thoughts about yourself, I should have held my temper. But no soul has challenged me in ages, and I'm out of practice. This entire behavior was so beneath me and so unworthy of what you deserve."

What I deserved was that tomb, the journal, the notes, the rotting things within.

The dark.

"No, my love." Monstrous paw to my cheek, a thumb tipped in a curling claw wiped my tears. "You deserve the sun. I don't care what God you think granted it to you. In fact, I should thank *him*, if it is indeed a man you see in God. For if you had been born human or Vampire, either way, once I had brought you back to my embrace, you would have lost the daylight. And now you can walk in both worlds, holding my hand."

A hand that dwarfed mine as he took it and brought it to his black lips.

"And you can look the angel while I look your devil." Another fervent kiss to my knuckles. "Lead me about by my nose."

Why was this breaking my heart? "But you *are* the devil."

"One who will learn to be good if only you'd love me."

Those eyes. Beast or man, no matter the shade or glow. I knew those eyes. "I do not want to talk to your Jesus, or sit with him, or know these things you know. I'm too tired."

"Lie down, my soul. Rest yourself under my wing. Sleep through the day, knowing I'm here." Beseeching tears fell from his unwavering, weighty gaze. "Forgive me my temper."

There was only one answer for all of this. "I will sleep under your wing, if you take me back to my tomb."

And leave me there to rot.

"No."

"Yes."

"Your soul would sing in sleep, and I'd hear and be driven mad by it." The monstrosity began to rise. "Even eternity entombed beside your corpse would not be enough to sate the beast. I need *you*. I need my soul. Order me about. Make demands. *Hurt me*. But thrive as you do so."

"You sound so—"

"In love?"

"Insane." Yet I said it with a teary laugh.

"Please. Let me beg. Let me grovel. Touch my face. See me."

And it should not have moved me as it did, but

his pleading stirred my belly enough to remind me to breathe. "I do see you. The serpent in the garden. And I have been waiting for the apple."

"It was a quince in the first telling of that tale. And there also was no garden nor Adam nor Eve, but I will pretend there was if it will appease you. Tell me to lie, and I will do so."

"Your truths are unbearable." And overwhelming, like walking over shards of glass.

"You are tired, my love. You are overwrought." It crept into the bed, the very bed I slinked toward the middle of to make room for the monster. "Sleep under my wing. Let me serve you."

He already stretched the massive appendage over the two of us, and I found myself having lain back upon the pillows. I accepted the dark. Because the rest of him did not touch me.

I dreamed of Coney Island.

I woke to smiles and joy. His joy.

Grit in my eyes, dog-tired as if I had not slept a wink, I wanted to turn my face into the pillow and hibernate for a year. Or a thousand.

"I think a long sleep would do you well." It had crept closer as I slumbered, flush to my frame and having pulled me to his chest. "Which I will grant you. But considering the mistakes I have already made, I would be remiss in failing to offer you the chance to see your daughter marry her love. I cannot let you regret it later."

The same daughter I had learned of only hours before. On my first date. Where all the actions I had always fantasized about had been delivered… along with many so out of my scope I had neglected to enjoy a moment of it.

"Seeing you—" Talons carded through my hair. "—it's hard to restrain my enthusiasm to have you home. To have you so close and so untouchable. *To crave*. Show me pity."

His pleadings had gone from forlorn to wide-eyed and silly, as had the expression on the face of the hideous thing. And I found that I had fallen for it, smirking no matter how I fought my lips.

"Three days? Three days, sleep. Three days, rest." The beast melted into the form of a man yet kept those wings. Though it had not kept the tatters of its clothing. "And on the third day, rise."

Yawning, the thought of a three-day-long sleep divine, my taunt came out a tease, "You really are Satan."

Wind settling over me, shutting out intrusive daylight, he hummed. "And you do so love to call me names."

Already half asleep, I turned my face into the pillow. "I never liked my own, so it's only fair."

The Relic

This made him laugh. "I'm not surprised. You were always extremely difficult to please."

Which was utterly incorrect. "All I ever wanted was kindness."

"And you were so starved you fail to see it when it's right before you. Even if the form offering it is hideous in your eyes."

When he sounded sad, it stirred me in a way I thoroughly disliked. But I was too tired to consider, already dreaming of evergreen forests when his awful lips scraped over my cheek.

"Three days, Pearl. Then I shall wake you with a feast."

On the third day, I rose.

In an entirely different room.

To the sound of church bells.

9
PEARL

The clothing hanging in a room called a *walk-in closet* was enviable. Gowns and blouses any working girl from my era would have spent their hard-earned pennies on. Out of date, yet still so beautiful I didn't want to touch in case I snagged the fabric.

A time capsule of the best years of my long life.

The 1920s had passed a century ago. Yet I'd clung to them and been indulged.

There was no mistaking that truth. Having been beaten, hung, drowned, shot, tortured, I still lived. And I was going to live forever. The more I imagined those immortals, those vampires, who wore mud or powdered wigs—how they failed to move forward out of insanity—the more I saw a reflection in myself.

The Relic

I saw it in the walk-in closet. In the cosmetics provided for me that were nothing like the advertisements on television. Cake mascara and rouge had not been used in decades, it seemed.

I saw it in my unwillingness to wear a bra, opting for an "old-fashioned" step-in.

I saw it each night when I dressed and looked in the mirror, my reflection, wearing clothes so beyond my means, so pretty, that any cigarette girl would have envied me.

Yet there were no cigarette girls anymore.

No one dressed this way save for themed parties.

And I was doing it by choice.

I—the hard worker, the adaptive employee—was stuck, stubborn, and willfully pouting about a world I had never been able to change. An ultimately pointless pursuit God would not approve of.

"I need *modern* clothing so I can get a job." Daring one last time, I touched one dress, a pale-pink number I admired and longed to deserve. "That restaurant with the terrible seafood platter had a sign in the window. They were looking for help. I could work there to pay for the clothes."

"I mean…" Vladislov sighed at my back, as if I had mentioned a topic he anticipated and loathed. "If you wish to work, it can be arranged. But the question of money? I have more wealth than the entire United States and continent of Europe combined."

"I like to work."

I felt the shrug in his words, imagined wings elongated in a careless flutter, though I knew he was in human form. "Many immortals do. I'd be the first to admit it's a great way to immerse oneself. But, may I counter your suggestion with one of my own?"

Turning so I might look at the person who'd woken me with a gentle kiss, to sacred bells of a church specially rung for me, to a priest speaking in French and a breakfast of *pain au chocolat*, I felt a bit beholden.

No.

I felt a sensation I'd never known outside of desperation. I felt grateful.

Gratitude had always come from begging just so I might survive. With this monster, gratitude came like it was a normal emotion.

"What do women wear? I've seen trousers. I'm not comfortable with that." Considering the final decade I remembered was all about women breaking free, my sentiment was silly. Women had already thrown off corsets, shortened their skirts, cut their hair.

Hell, I had cut mine!

Hell?

The Relic

I began to laugh. As did my host.

"Husband." A smooth voice paired with a smooth hand down my arm. "I am your husband, not your host."

Something in me bantered easily, was playful in a way I had never been with a man. "But we're not married."

"My sweet soul, if a ceremony would please you, I'll have us 'wed' in the grandest of fashions. A virginal white gown, veil trailing to be held by one hundred attendants."

Chilling as quickly as I had warmed, I thought of only one word. The one that stung. "I'm not virginal."

He pulled down the outdated dress I liked most, turning me to hold it before my frame. "In every possible way, you are a pure virgin deserving the crown of a queen… even if you want to hostess at a restaurant or wash dishes in a kitchen."

When he talked in such a way, I would blush. Felt it creeping up my cheek as I pretended to admire the upheld, beautiful dress instead of meeting his eye. "You mentioned a suggestion?"

"University." The tip of his human finger tapped my nose. "Join a sorority, eat pizza, and drink beer, go to parties and make friends. Take classes and expand the mind I already recognize as brilliant. Any subject can be at your fingertips. Work if you wish, but consider that study will be time-consuming. And I must be fair in stating that you will need tutelage before you might be admitted. I have a collection of wise minds ready to teach you, which might eat up years until you can quote Plato as well as you quote Psalms."

"You are teasing me." He had to be. I was dumber than a rock. At least fifteen of my former employers had said so.

"Uh, they are so lucky they are already dead." A peck landed on my lips between his complaints. "Wear this pink number tonight. We can stay in and watch a modern movie if you want to leap forward into what's trending now. If you're feeling daring, we can watch *the movie* that has an entire planet of women overjoyed and salivating."

"But we're only at 1959." Jumping ahead seemed forbidden! Yet at the same time… was there really any point in postponing the inevitable. What did women these days watch? I would see their mannerisms and clothes. Hairstyles, cosmetic trends. Perhaps this was the best first step. "I would like to see this movie."

Gathering up the underthings to match the 1920s costume, Vladislov said, "It will be very modern. I think the word might be risqué."

"Women in the 1920s were very modern. They could vote!" And indeed that had made me very worried in that age. For so much violence was brought down upon those females who wanted a voice. And I had not agreed, as women were God's flawed creation. But then I'd seen a cultural renaissance... a phrase I overheard from a guest at the Supper Club and had looked up at the library.

So why not watch this movie? Why not wear the clothes?

But no trousers!

Even in my era, those looked improper.

"How brave you are, my soul!" Laughing, Vladislov wrapped an arm around me. "All of this will be removed and replaced. No need to look at me that way. It will be saved for parties or your whim. Yet I will contradict one fashion statement from the years you're considering. Bras are overrated. I'll cover you in lace, in satin, in silk, but please, I beg you, my darling, do not confine such perfect breasts in a bra."

Nipples tightening at their mere mention, I pulled the house coat tighter around my chest. "What do women sleep in?"

His eyebrows bounced. "In the nude, of course."

"You're lying..."

"Fine..." He sighed as if I were extremely troublesome for failing to take the bait. "Nightgowns, teddies, lingerie, pajamas. And yes, some do prefer to sleep naked. If I have a vote, I vote naked. You'd glow wearing nothing but moonlight."

"You're too forward." I would have never said that to a patron as I sold cigarettes. I would have let him slather me with innuendo and grab my breast or rump. But I said it now, because I was no longer a cigarette girl. I was to be a modern woman of a new century. "It makes me uncomfortable."

Grinning, he leaned close enough to take a deep breath of me. "Uncomfortable is not the right word. It makes you nervous, because it excites you."

Heart pounding, strange fluttery feelings in my belly, I closed my eyes and collected my thoughts. Warmed where his heat poured into me. Oddly breathless when he ran his nose over my hair.

Full-on shivering when he whispered at my ear, "I would be very gentle, immensely careful, if you would only let me kiss you."

A kiss? Was there really any harm? My lips already felt plump, tingled with the thought of it.

It was all I could do not to touch them.

Yet he pulled away, eyes warm and smile soft. "But not yet. First, let's watch this film and see just what makes the modern woman tick."

Hand going to the tie of my robe, he pulled the knot before I might react. Off went my robe, followed with a flourish of my cotton nightgown until I was naked, gaping, and reaching out for anything to cover myself.

Chin in his hand, he cocked his head and considered. "Perfect breasts. Perfect sex. Please don't have your pubic hair ripped out the way women do these days. I love those beautifully scented, soft curls just as they are."

Already stepping into my underthings, red up to my ears, I tripped once I grasped what he said. "Women remove... that hair? Why?"

"Cunnilingus. Though the fashion fluctuates decade to decade, in these times, many men complain when their partner likes to be licked between her thighs and the lady's sex is in the natural state. Call me old fashioned, but I disagree. I want to smell and feel all of you."

My breasts were covered in thin satin, and after I snatched the pink dress from my tormentor, my body was reasonably concealed. But I felt the oddest pulsating warmth between my legs. And by the way Vladislov winked and took another deep breath, I realized he could smell it.

"I can, and your arousal smells divine. I bet you taste like honey."

And I was growing offended to be so outmatched. "Such talk is for husbands and wives!"

"As we are married, I knew you'd like it." Hooking my arm through his, he led me stumbling from the closet. "But enough verbal foreplay. Let's go watch this film the female population is aflutter over."

"I don't trust you one bit. I've changed my mind about the movie."

"Too late!" As if playfully offended, he mimicked a wound to his heart. "Besides, I do not decide what women like. Look on social media and see the unrelenting posts about this film. You want to immerse yourself in the modern woman's psyche, there is no better jumping off point."

Waltzed through the rooms, spun until my legs caught the sofa, I plopped down on the cushion. Vladislov stretching out at my side, remote in hand.

His fingers moved faster than the program might load, which I could sense annoyed him, as he was trying so hard to play cool and not pin me in place.

The film began, looking *so real* compared to films from the 50s—like standing right there with the actors. The sound of waves crashing was so fresh that I was enraptured with this *magic*.

A girl taken captive by a handsome, evil man. One who swears she will fall in love with him.

I don't think my jaw closed the entire rest of the film. Every moral part of me knew I needed to look away, but they were naked! How could I have known the brazen filth that women relished in these days?

The Relic

So beyond what I had anticipated... the beautiful woman seduced the man who caught her in his web. She took his member into her mouth!

Oh lord! He licked her between her legs!

Cunnilingus Vladislov had teased me about, though she was hairless—as he had also mentioned.

And when they made love—if the violence in which they took one another's body could be called that—she enjoyed it.

Women enjoyed sex?

"Very much so, Pearl. Modern women have taken sexual control of their bodies and enjoy the act even more than the man in many instances."

"I don't understand this."

How the villain showered the wanton captive with praise.

How she adored him, despite the fact that he kidnapped... stolen her away.

I'd been stolen and locked in a crypt.

I'd felt a cock thrust in me, known the tearing of delicate tissues. Hated all of it.

I had climaxed with a scream just as the actress continued to do.

But her cries were of joy.

I had never been sated in such a way.

And seeing this...

It made me sad.

Frustrated.

Angry.

Disgustingly eager.

Did women really like these things?

On a couch, in a room I had never seen, I sat beside a character from all human nightmares and grew confused at the pulse growing between my legs each time the actors coupled.

"I don't understand." But I understood enough to grasp why Vladislov moved to kneel before me. Why he was gently pushing up my skirt, inserting his frame between my weakening knees.

Parting me so the slit in my step-in might be found and dark curls exposed.

And I could not wrap my mind around the fact that I was allowing it.

Holding my eyes, his touch slowly moving up my inner thigh, he said, "That gentle kiss I promised. I'd like to give it to you now."

"I won't like it." Not the way the woman did on screen. Never like that.

His fingertips reached my undergarment's opening, pulling it wide to expose even more of me. "Then I'll stop."

One could say the first touch of his lips in that forbidden place was indeed chaste. Soft pressure at the apex of my sex, right where I tingled the most.

Pressing my head back into the couch cushions,

I gasped. Hips rocking so I might know more, just like the woman on the screen had done.

And more, I was given.

I don't know if his tongue was forked, but it was evil through and through as the demon sluiced through my juices to flick at my lower lips. To strum a delicious knot of pleasure above my hungry opening.

There was nothing shy or modest in how he *kissed* me. Nothing innocent. Nose, chin, mouth, tongue, even teeth played me like a song.

And I did scream, bucking and wild and someone else entirely, climaxing with shaking legs within minutes.

It was as if I had finally been exorcised of a demon.

Breathless as he redoubled his efforts and pierced me with a tongue I knew was black, fat, and far longer than any human tongue. Undulating that thing within me, his nose nudging the bead where all sensation centered, I screamed again.

And again.

And again.

I was *kissed* until the sun rose. Until my voice was gone and my senses were muddled by pleasure.

And then the man pulled back, licking his smiling lips with a tongue more dangerous than sin. Climbing over where I was spent, where I realized I had been brazenly clutching at my own breast and pinching the aching nipple.

He murmured, "Better than honey," kissing me to share the flavor of what he dined on throughout an entire night.

I tasted nothing like honey, but I found his tongue in my mouth delicious. His weight on my body divine.

Nipping his way across my jaw, he whispered the ultimate temptation, "We could make love in the sunlight. Gentle and slow."

Perhaps we could....

My final thought before exhaustion and an unnatural sense of relaxation took me away.

10

VLADISLOV

Laying her in her new bed, in this new country, in this fresh start, I knew my soul wouldn't wake until sunset. Not after the *progress* we had made… a dozen times or more.

She had not believed she would enjoy my tongue between her legs in her past life either. The first time had been quite a violent tussle. This time, all it required was some sensational media.

Bless the makers of softcore porn for women. I'd have them all changed so more movies of that nature might be produced and I might get the pleasure of eating pussy from dusk to daybreak again.

A vampire armada of smut makers! Ha!

Just wait until my queen viewed a real-life orgy. I bet she'd bob up and down my cock all night after furious blushing and five minutes of pretending not to look.

Was it too soon to throw her that style of party?

Yes.

I sighed, willing to press progress even if I couldn't have my orgy. It was not too soon to strip her out of those clothes and let her know the glory of soft sheets on bare skin. Which would get me in a bit of trouble when she woke, especially as I would be just as naked and pressed flush against her.

There was no helping my dripping erection, so that too she would experience and muse over.

How delicious her musings were.

What a pity I had not been able to read her thoughts in her past life. Had I been able to, I could have been far more cunning and much less violent with my jewel. She might have loved me even more.

I might not have had to threaten the life of the very baby whose delivery had drained her to the point of death. I might not have threatened to kill it if she had not made the oath that would bring her back to me.

A child I could not bear to look at as it grew. Who outlived all his brothers and took my throne when I wandered off to make the world bleed for leaving me soulless and desolate—the great, great, great, great, many more greats grandfather of Darius.

In whom, after a thousand years, I'd tried to make amends.

Considering Darius' head was now on a pike and my soul was afraid of the pleasure due her, I should have killed that baby after all—horrible thing that tore its way out of the only creature in existence worth anything.

I supposed my love's rebirth was a boon in the fact that she would remember none of this. And it would be thousands of years before she might gain the ability to pry into my thoughts and see what I'd done. By then she would be hopelessly tied to me, utterly in love. Devoted as I was to her.

Just lying near her made me ache.

I would give her physical pleasure for a thousand years and seek none for myself if only to please her. Though it might make my pants fit a bit oddly walking around with a constant erection. Perhaps codpieces might come back into style?

Nestling said erection between the warm buttocks of a sex-addled, drowsing daywalker, I covered us both with one wing. This too she would grow accustomed to, for I could not resist the need to do it.

The need.

Holding her in such a way fed me more than thoughts of fucking her. Though, there was no question I very much longed to plow her into oblivion. I could come all over her beautiful backside right now if I just let my mind wander into fun thoughts.

But waking up with dried semen on her back, already naked and in my arms, would absolutely make her mad. She might slap me.

I might like it.

And... it was too late. Like an untried boy, I had just spurt where I may or may not have been rocking myself against soft buttocks.

If I were to just... rub the come in, what was the harm in that?

Massages were very popular in this era. If she woke, I'd simply tell her I was trying to keep up with the times.

And still, she'd slap me.

It would be worth it.

Considering I was already hard again, I could keep this massage tactic up all night. Imagine how rested she would be when she woke. If I had a bath prepared, she would hop right to it in her modesty before really analyzing the situation.

Filling it with bubbles like the scene in the movie might even show her how adept I am in noticing what intrigues her.

Perhaps no bubbles, but a tub full of warm, immortal blood?

There were plenty of vampires in my prisons who were unworthy to pass her lips, but good as a blood bag to be tapped to luxuriate her skin. It would be a very vampire-y thing to do. Her first step into embracing her other half.

I'd be her servant, properly clothed with a toga around my hips, feeding her grapes and sips of blood straight from the vein while she soaked.

Three spurts of come on my sleeping wife's back was probably the limit I might get away with before the sheets turned crusty. Hand to my cock, pulling forth the greatest release of the night, I did my best to angle more of it at me than at the sweet globes of her pale ass.

I really was such a liar.

What man in his right mind would not come all over so plump an ass?

Absolutely sane, I lifted my wing enough to see the creamy globs dripping toward her more intimate area, salivating to lick her clean, and groaned.

Heaven was Hell, and in my arms slept the true ruler of the underworld. Tormenting me with her beauty, her goodness, her scrumptious tits and ass. I was Hades, and she was Persephone, except in the real tale, there was no Demeter to steal her away from me for half the seasons. And now death could not touch her.

She was mine!

Skin black and burning, talons lengthening as my hands grew and my body bulged with strength, I cupped her flesh and seared my seed into soft skin. A bit frenzied in the art of manipulating muscle into bliss.

Many hours had already passed, the tub of blood had been prepared at my mental bidding, and beautiful blue eyes opened, wide with shock to see that, no, I did not cradle her and have her covered in my wing. I knelt over her, massive wingspan possessively closing out the setting sun, my touch kneading her body as yet another throbbing erection dripped onto her belly.

Balls tight to my shaft, they churned to release, yet I ignored them to wish her good evening. "How did you rest, my love?"

Speechless from my attention, or maybe from the wide-eyed stare at my bobbing cock, Pearl failed to reply.

"There is no need to be frightened of your husband's body." The arm I had been stroking, I drew my kneading grip down her limb and brought her hand to hover over my erection. "You can touch me if you want to. Explore me and know you are safe. I will not have sex with you until you ask me to."

Had that been too similar to the line in yesterday's film?

There was something new in her at that moment.

Terror, yes, but also bite. "And when you do, what happens then?"

That one stumped me. "I suppose it depends on what you're in the mood for next."

"Will you make me put my mouth on you like —" She swallowed, flushed skin going pale. Thoughts of Darius and his debauchery were in her mind, but it was the film she referred to. "—like the man in the movie did to his *wife*."

This, I could work with.

Flipping her over before she might scream or fight back, I put her in the exact position the actor had first fucked his captive. Draping my body over her back, I settled my wings to embrace us and took the lobe of her ear in my teeth. "He did this to her as well. Fucked her while her hands were chained to the headboard."

I did not penetrate, but I did let my organ smooth through her folds in a long, slow stroke I hoped would entice arousal and not screams.

"My love, is it not better to jump into the water and swim? Toeing the shore will drive you mad."

Shaking so hard I could hear her teeth chatter, Pearl stopped me in my tracks. "Don't."

But this was not the time for retreat. There was a reason I had conquered the known world time and again. I would conquer this too. "I'm asking for you to trust me."

And I scythed the long, aching length of my penis again between her folds. And again. As I cooed and stroked her, as my wings warmed her from her fear-inspired chill.

I mimicked the act of fucking without actually penetrating my darling one. Offering us both a taste of pleasure until she began to pant and the muscles I worked to caress all night began to relax. Her head to the mattress, her ass in the air. My breath at her ear, and my cock stroking her clit, I took my time. And in time, she took her pleasure.

But it would not be enough to send her to bliss.

If she wanted that, she'd have to ask.

And I could hump her gorgeous ass for all eternity. Suffer with her.

The sun rose, and though her hips had begun to squirm in an attempt to get the friction her body desperately needed for release, she didn't ask.

So I showed mercy.

Slinking down her body, taking her hips in hand, I brought her swollen sex to my mouth and let her experience the art of eating pussy from another angle. One that let me delve my tongue deep, tease her anus. Flatter her clit with praise.

Screaming my name, she came.

A thing she had not even dared the night before. Progress indeed!

Progress enough that I crossed the threshold with questionable permission, while she was dazed and assumed the perfect position to end this standoff.

Cockhead to slit, I pressed in.

Knowing I was too big in my true form, I took astounding care and sealed our fates with the truth of the matter.

"You called for me." At the perfect shell of her ear, I growled like the animal I was.

And gained another inch.

Permission enough.

Battle won.

It took almost an hour, a great deal of caresses, incessant circles over her clit, and compliments in every language man had ever spoken before I was fully seated in my wife's cunt.

In which time she had come apart on my cock four times, unable to resist pushing back against my intrusion and impaling herself as her channel sucked at my meat and adapted.

My sword was sheathed in perfect, tight fire.

The beauty of her pussy stretched around me. Sound and pulsating. Wet and welcoming.

The very first time I had taken my wife in ages long past, I'd had to oil my cock to facilitate a struggling penetration. Now, she was wet for me. Now, I was home.

"I love you." I said it a thousand times or more, felt it where my soul had been returned to me.

I wept, rocking my hips to seek that perfect embrace over and over.

Exactly how I desired to spend the rest of eternity.

Yet ultimate bliss could not be held at bay forever. My darling, overwrought, screamed into her pillow, clenched down around my member in a series of rippling tugs, physically demanding seed as her orgasm blossomed.

As her eternal slave, I could do nothing but comply.

She drained me dry, my roar shaking the walls.

When it was over, when I carefully pulled out in smiling satisfaction to see the sticky cream flooding her contracting channel, I knew a child would be made before the year was out… and that she would love me for it.

11

PEARL

It was over...

Every part of me oversensitive to the point I would combust if he attempted to pleasure me further. Hand pressed between my legs, I turned my back to the beast and stared at the wall —the plaster now cracked from the monstrous howl that had set the building to quake.

"There is no need to hold my seed in, my soul." Settling at my back, draping my body in that wing, it snuggled me. "I can give you more any time you wish. Rest with me for a short while, then I have a surprise! The first of many."

I couldn't imagine what could possibly be more surprising than what had just taken place.

"I feel as if a feast is in order to celebrate! Oh,

sweet wife, you have given me such a gift that I cannot even fathom how to adore you best."

Given him?

Wife?

Was I now more the wife he believed me to be because I had let him rut me? Because I had shamelessly shut my eyes to the monster on my back and abandoned all reason.

"I won't always be ugly to you. A pure heart like yours will learn to love me for who I am and not the shell I wear." He kissed my neck, lightly scraping his fangs on my flesh. "I know this, because I once was beautiful, and you didn't love me for my beauty as all other women did. It was my spirit that drew you. Even if I were to wear that form again, beauty would never earn you."

When his bite punched through delicate tissue, a great jaw holding my throat, it wasn't pain I felt.

Only a sip was taken.

"To drink from the throat of another immortal is only done between those who are excessively intimate. It's practically our only taboo." Licking at the twin wounds that were already closing, he hummed out a great contented breath. "My throat is yours."

"I don't want your throat." I don't know why I said it, or why my voice held such vindictiveness. But I felt a great need to hurt the beast. Or hurt myself.

Rolling me to my back so he might make me look at him—or perhaps he wanted to look at me, my body was planted between two massive arms. "Once upon a time, you wanted my throat. Held a knife to it on our wedding night, would have slit me ear to ear had you the talent for it. I've often wondered if it was your magic that made us what we became, our oath, or my will alone. But blood? It always comes back to blood."

And if I had that knife now?

Would I take the throat he bared?

Try to kill the monster who had pulled me from my grave, cared for me, clothed me, fed me, fucked me? Twice damned was I, meeting his gaze and hazarding a question. "Why did I try to slit your throat?"

"You didn't want to be queen, though you were born the jewel of the kingdom." The beast looked lost in memory. "Raised in seclusion, you'd never interacted with any man beyond our father. Who spoiled you to a fault and loved you more than our sisters. And it was not just for your great beauty. It was for your tenacity and will to have your way. The greatest queens never hunger for the duty. They must be tamed. When you tried to kill me, I'd never been more in love."

"That sounds sick." Truly sickening.

Careful of his talons, Vladislov cupped my

cheek. "There is nothing sick in love. You found joy in freedom, in my body, in my obsession, and even in your duty."

Joy might not be the emotion I would equate with what had just happened. Unable to decide if I had tricked myself, or he had fooled me, or if I really was a whore willing to take the cock of a demon having been tempted with little more than a tickle between the legs.

What bothered me most was that if he had asked me, I would not have said yes.

"Which is precisely why I didn't ask. You called out my name in need, and I gave you what you *needed*. It was an ask enough."

How he could play at words, and actions, and move me at his whim…

Laughing, the beast contradicted my concerns. "It's the other way around. I cannot think but for you. Watch your every minuscule movement, listen to your heartbeat, see you fed, clothed, cared for… bedded. I am your slave."

"Then I order you to leave me forever."

Laughter turned to so pained an expression my heart ached to see it.

He spilled a tear. "I would not go, because you are incapable of such cruelty."

"I'm sorry." Why I said it, or why I meant it, I could not even begin to contemplate.

Boxed in by his arms, arms that were muscular in ways no creature should be, solemn as the grave, Vladislov said, "I would make love to you again, face to face, before we bathe. I want you to see me when you feel beauty, and know that I see you."

My ardor had cooled, yet the seed between my legs was slippery enough for seeking fingers to play in when his knee moved to separate my thighs.

With an arch, my body refused the command of my thoughts. And though I fought to keep my legs closed, it did not take long for his weight to settle between them. The first thrust stole my breath, dragging over something inside me that drew out a shameless moan.

Just as he had commanded, I witnessed his pleasure as he took my body. Eyes roving from bouncing breasts, to my parted lips. And where his eyes went, his mouth followed.

Tongue twisting with mine, fingers dancing over my breasts, I submitted as a wife submits to her husband. Locking my ankles at his back, taking all he would give me.

As Adam took Eve in the garden.

Hideous as he was, every bit of me burned. But not with shame as it should have. With passion when I was given what my corrupted body craved. My world turned to pure white when he sliced his throat and set it to my mouth.

I drank as he filled me, coming so violently that had he been human, I would have accidentally killed him.

In the panting aftermath, whatever surprise he had planned was forgotten. The night spent entwined while I came apart under beating wings, a snake-like tongue, and eyes full of adoration that moved me.

And frightened me in equal measure.

The sun rose, the sun set, over and over while I learned the ways of pleasure. It was not until I was straddling the beasts, riding at my pace while I sang out my release that I was shown mercy.

Exhaustion left me crumpled on his chest, sleep winning over even as I felt more of his seed pumping inside me.

I dreamed of Jesus in the desert and forty days of a dark winged angel trying to talk sense into his son.

12

VLADISLOV

The bloodbath was not a hit with my bride. And in all fairness to my intention, was unfair in itself. After all, I offered candlelight, flowers in abundance, snacks… a cake! But she would not put a toe in the tub.

Pearl even tried to yank her hand from where our fingers were entwined… as if I'd let her run off and possibly hurt herself in an unwarranted panic.

Human in form and lighthearted in tone, I attempted to smooth ruffled feathers. "The mass murder playing in such detail through you mind did not take place. Every drop was donated. All immortal, all happy to indulge their queen in a fun… let's call it… *tradition*."

Which was not exactly dishonest. Those immortals drained for the event really were happy to be thrown a snack so I might plump my withered prisoners up again for future bath time fun. But the miniscule details were unimportant. "It's the perfect temperature, enhanced with essential oils, full of petals to slip against your skin, and the finest salts to soothe your aches. Best to get in now before it begins to curdle. Do you want our people to be sad to hear their gift was wasted?"

But she was not budging no matter how gentle my voice or touch.

The expression of horror on her face was not melting into gratitude.

I could work on that. Lips stretching in a smile that displayed the fangs Vampirekind was known for, I reached for a golden dome, sweeping it from a beautiful offering with a silly flourish. "I have chocolate for you. Parisian delicacies," the words sung as I tempted her with a bite of sweets.

Though her nostrils flared at the aroma of so much decadence, under her breath, she muttered, "This is sin."

My own muttering was far less tragic and far more eye-rollingly annoyed. "Wasting it might be."

Okay, so this was the third tub I had filled over the last few days of rigorously fucking my bride. But what had swirled down the drain was not wasted *exactly*. It was a practice run to make sure that *this* tub was perfect. Even the candlelight had been arranged just so to play off the quickly setting sun. A pretty stage, a room inviting my timid bride to embrace the heritage that had been denied her.

What point was there in hesitation? My Pearl just needed a little mental nudge. "Humans have bathed in milk for as long as I have walked this earth. Does milk not come from animals? Yes, it's generally used for sustenance, but it also softens the skin and is enjoyed as a luxury. You ingest immortal blood—" I gave her a roguish wink, growing hard just at the thought of it. "—and we both know I'm your favorite snack. The only difference here is perspective."

Opening her mouth as if to argue, like a true gentleman, I put a finger to her lips and saved her the trouble. "I'm right, of course. So in you go."

Where my touch traced her kiss-swollen lips, she frowned. "I wouldn't want to take a bath in milk either. I'd hardly had the funds to taste it before you woke me up from the nightmare." Visibly shuddering, my darling bride grimaced, because somewhere deep in her very scarred psyche, a bubble of awfulness I refused to pop grew. It grew, and it teased at the scars Darius had dug into her mind.

Everything that had been done, taken, rewritten,

molded, concealed... it was in there. It clamored. Someday, it would make her a monster in need of checking. Which was why my gentle Pearl needed taming and self-acceptance.

I'd make her a God... and she might make the whole world pay for it.

Maybe the world deserved what they created—Vampire, human, Daywalker, and all the other monsters creeping along the earth's crust.

Pupils dilating, Pearl stared down at the warmed tub. "I can hear the screams."

Yes, she could. But they were her screams. Buried and in need of exorcism. Hand to my heart, I set my obsessive, complete, unbreakable love plain on my face. "On my honor, no contributor to your warm bath died."

There was really no point in bringing up the human livestock that had gone into fattening up the donating immortals... considering the unraveling mental state before me. Their blood was not technically in the tub, so it didn't matter. The effort, the two previously drained tubs, and the volume—a cool hundred humans had most likely been eaten. But they would have been eaten anyway. Just like cows were butchered in messy slaughterhouses en masse.

Pools of scintillating immortal blood, romantic moments of this nature, were not produced from mass hunting of monkeys on the streets. The humans involved had been taken from pens all over my worldwide domain. And not even the good bloodlines. Those fed to immortal prisoners were waste product. Hardly edible.

But again, that was neither here nor there. Overthinking wasn't going to get my bride into that tub. The racing echo of her heart, the ripples of her mind, the little twitches all over her body—nothing that night was going to get her into the tub.

I had misstepped.

I had conquered nations.

Therefore, I knew every mistake held the seed of an even better victory. "Pearl, I'm sorry."

"Why?" How confused she was. How disarmed. Horrified, dangerous, full of my strength and learning her own. The very essence of her trapped in the mind of a stunted seventy-year-old. An infant, considering our longevity.

A survivor whose fangs would grow back sharper than they had ever been before.

It wasn't her hesitation or the newness of the situation. It was a fundamental, lingering complaint. My Pearl was offended, yet she didn't comprehend why. My vicious bride reborn was angry, but not with me.

Even in that moment, her mind wrestled with the joy she found in our physical pleasure. The pain

Darius had stripped from her. The pain he had left her with.

The endless slog of her life until, in a state of terror, she had finally found other beings like her.

The unfairness.

A bath of blood.

A cracked porcelain sink she had vomited crimson poison into after ripping the throat of Chadwick Parker on that snowy night in 1927. The unfairness of the world and the fact that a thing she regarded as the antithesis of the Christian God was the only creature to show her kindness.

Her mind screamed. Her face became that of stone.

The impassive visage of an angry queen.

"I won't go in your tub." What a voice she could wield when she dug it out.

What a woman.

She challenged me. Me? A creature of her worst nightmares. Her bridegroom. A bat of my eyelash and she would implode.

The things Darius had done to her were nothing compared to a true imagination.

There were vast, innumerable, disturbing, elegant reasons I was feared the world over. Why I had earned so many monikers.

There were reasons I was also beloved. *The*

morning star. The most beautiful creature to walk the earth.

The most hideous.

Running my fingertips through her tousled hair, my heart aching with love, I gave her truth. "I can have the building burned to the ground so your eyes might never lay upon this room again."

Waspish, she threw off my touch and crossed her arms under perfect breasts. Plumped, delicious skin I might never have my fill of was distracting beyond belief. But I kept my eyes on hers, even as she challenged, "You can't burn a building down because I don't like something in it!"

"Of course I can." Seriously, starting fires was really easy. The amount of cities I had sacked....

I mean, really. If mankind had any concept of the civilizations I had crushed into powder—metallurgy, plumbing, technology—the entirety of documented history would be upended.

But it all had come too soon when the rest of the world was still picking fleas from their hair.

And the best minds were welcome to join my family. To become my children, of a sort.

Da Vinci still painted hidden works when he was not unraveling astrophysics. The *human* lives that child of mine has suffered. Because living as a human is suffering. Especially to the brilliant.

"Vladislov"—had she just spoken my name?—"I dreamed of your time in the desert. He warned you. You warned him. Neither father nor son listened."

Taking her chin in my hand, struggling to remain human in appearance when I was so deeply affected, I said, "The tub, Pearl. We can talk of my indiscretion while I was awaiting your rebirth later."

"Would he hate me?" And the question was bare to me—I could see it plain as moonlight. Would he hate her for what had been done to her?

"He will love you." Though it had to be said, "You may not love your Jesus in return. In fact, you may resent him. So much hinges on the legacy he never comprehended, and I warned the boy. The second coming will never be what humans have imagined. It won't be at all. He is unloved no matter how he represents himself through the ages. "Even now, he stands in the American Senate proffering love and change. Jewish, ethical, strongly beloved by a loud minority, threatened and quashed by a more powerful majority. No different than his early years."

"You said he was in Brazil?"

"Your daughter is getting married to the soldier who ripped your fangs from your skull tomorrow evening." My granddaughter, my stepdaughter—my weak yet stronger than many, oddly bound offspring. "She too is now free of Darius. Would you like to witness her find peace?"

So much regret passed through the mind before me. Flashes of how Pearl had seen humans hold and nurse their babies. How she had no memory of feeling kicks behind her ribs or suckling. How she had been ripped to shreds.

"As the tub is getting cold, might I suggest you offer the experience to a friend? We'll go out to dinner. You find a place on the Yelp. Any city, and we can be there in a flash."

"What would someone wear to a wedding these days? Pants?" How she despised trousers on women! It was endearingly adorable. But, those were tears gathering in her eyes.

Pearl had not yet accepted the facts. "You could show up naked if you wanted to. You're my queen."

The idea of a child was still spinning in her mind. Proving I was once again right for seeking to impregnate her for her own joy.

Wide, wet eyes met mine. "If I took the bath, would she like me more?"

This desire for acceptance was going to be a problem. One I had overcome with countless generations of offspring. "No."

Pearl's heart slowed. "I shouldn't go."

Tired of pretending the human form, my arms

grew black as pitch. I displayed all of me. Every last, hideous bit.

Soothing my wife, claws delicate as the traced skin, I said, "She doesn't know who you are. You will arrive as only my guest. She needs that now Later, she will need you."

13

PEARL

I'd never attended a wedding, though I had seen some in films and read about them in the papers. Not that I had much basis for comparison, but it would seem vampire weddings were not much different than human ones at first glance. Formally dressed and greeting one another with elaborate displays of affection, guests chatted. Other guests avoided one another, offering their counterpart little more than an icy stare.

It reminded me of the Supper Club: the cliques, the grandeur. The affection and the cruelty.

Vladislov had seen me lavishly dressed. Blood-red so bright it seemed garish to my tastes. I stood out like a sore thumb in a gown fit for a queen. Enough jewels hung from my throat and dripped from my ears that the weight of them was uncomfortable.

The choker must have been ancient, the style odd and the metal imperfect. It circled my throat, from collarbones to jaw. It pinched.

But how he had smiled to drape them around my neck, explaining, "Our kind does not expose the throat at public events. It's considered… uncultured. Though, if I might say so, the true motivation behind the collars is fear. The jewels are armor. The only bare throat you will see tonight is that of the bride and groom. If someone should expose themselves to you, do not drink."

No soul had done such a thing at Vladislov's party. "Why would someone do that?"

"Because you smell of sunshine, and all Vampires desire the use of a Daywalker. Stay by my side," he teased, "or one of the less wise might just try to snatch you away."

I was going to be sick. Already nervous to see the child I'd never known—one I had been warned would dislike me at first glance. One I was not to speak with, not on her day. After all, I had been reminded over and over that we had eternity to thaw the ice.

These instructions, given by a monster in the shape of a man, were not for Jade's benefit. They were for mine. Vladislov didn't want to see me hurt by what would be obvious and public rejection. I didn't need to read his mind to grasp that fact.

From the way he spoke as he decked me in jewels that could buy kingdoms, I also wondered if he cared for Jade at all.

As if to defend himself from my thoughts, his fingers stilled, and his eyes turned up to mine. "I find your daughter, my granddaughter… refreshing. Never forget that I gave her a kingdom, though she is difficult and looks too much like her father."

Which made me all the more nervous. Darius was my living nightmare.

A light peck landed on my lips. "She has your eyes, though the blue turned red when I gave her the throne. Look there and you will see yourself. She has your resilience and your strength. Darius was always a weakling in a strong body."

Red eyes? Why was I even going to this wedding?

"She's your daughter. She's getting married. You will regret it for eternity if you miss it out of unfounded shyness. Think in eons, Pearl. One day, you will be her friend. One day, she will be grateful you made the effort. That day will not be today. Again, do not speak to her."

"And her fiancé?" I remembered the pale-haired angel who'd torn out my fangs, broken my jaw, and dumped me at the foot of a despotic evil.

"Malcom knows that if he approaches, I will kill him. Which would ruin the wedding." He said it so lightly, as if so wild a declaration it were nothing at all.

"My daughter loves him. You told me he led you to where I…." I didn't have a name for that room or for what had happened in it. "I'm not so stupid that I don't understand why he—"

Echoing my earlier thoughts, Vladislov showed enough temper that his whole form twitched as if he fought to maintain it. "Ripped out your beautiful fangs, broke your jaw, and delivered you to Darius so he might play his games with you when you should have been immediately brought to me?"

I could already see the seams stretching, patting his chest as if to hold back the beast and its wings. "You'll rip your fine clothes if you don't take a deep breath."

My warning only earned me a poke on the forehead. "If you could only see the mess in here. I tolerate Malcom out of some misplaced fondness for Jade. I tolerate him, because he was loyal. But I can clearly see what he did to my wife. How terrified you were, the pain it caused. Why should I care if it was done in service?"

"You don't get to have an opinion about it. That's why. It was done to me." Had those words just come out of my mouth?

"Consider me chastened." And tamed. He went from smoking devil to playful puppy. Kissing my lips in little nips and calling me stunning as his fingers found my nipple through the daringly low cut bodice of my ridiculous dress. "Before we go, can I fuck you on the counter? In this dress, just like this? I want to know I'm leaking down your leg while peasants approach and fools think to negotiate."

It was less of a question and more of a prayer. Already, he'd begun bunching up my voluminous skirt, the edge of the dressing room's marble counter at my thighs. Moving faster than my eyes might register, he pulled himself from his trousers, uncaring that his pants fell to his ankles, and was in.

In me.

The pinching fetters of so many stones around my neck, the initial cramp when something too big filled a place that seemed incessantly wet. I found bliss.

He fucked me. Right there as I clung and gasped.

Coming too soon, earning cruel laughter from an incessantly hard bull, I braced. Because there was always more.

So much so that we were late for the gathering. My hair, once beautiful, was a half-fallen mess. And yes, he was dripping down my leg.

Not yet recovered from the bending world that went from dressing room to riverside wedding, I stumbled. I clung.

I knew I was ridiculous.

Many approached my guardian.

"Husband," he whispered at my ear, giving it a lick despite the audience of immortals.

Languages were spoken that I didn't know. Addresses were made, even to me—polite, tolerant nods in many cases. Wide-mouthed grins in others.

Fangs were on full display, glittering in the moonlight.

Though when I forced a smile in reply, I saw how vampire eyes went straight to my stumped incisors. There were looks of pity, looks of disgust.

"The groom tore them out himself!" Vladislov chuckled, though the very tone of his laughter was menace.

Under my breath, I tried to stop him. "Vladislov!"

"She asked me not to kill him." My less than delightful companion eased nearer the latest supplicant. "But she never asked me to spare you. Leave."

A man I hardly noticed may as well have pissed himself, vanishing into the night as if he'd never been there.

Could this be more uncomfortable? "That wasn't funny."

"He looked at your throat." As if that was explanation enough.

Like a king approaching his throne, Vladislov entered the fray, literally dragging me into the masses. Tripping over my skirt, one arm flailed, and a spray of glowing, white flowers began to fall.

Caught before the crash by Maya. Who gave me a wink before a goddess in the flesh moved back into the crowd. I didn't have a chance to say thank you.

"I've known Maya for thousands of years. Believe me when I say, she is genuine, unforgiving, and willing to spend her time getting to know you. That is rare." With a pout on his lips, my face red and posture shrinking, I heard him add, "I suspect you will be fast friends and that I will be very jealous."

"Can you please stop? Just stop, Vlad!"

He didn't stop, but all around us did. It was as if time froze, the stillness of all in attendance. A mercenary indrawn breath to see what would happen next.

"For you, my bride, anything." Leaning down to press a kiss to my cheek, he added, "I'm sorry."

Everyone turned my way. A chilling unison of movement. A sea of people, of costume, of fanfare. Of years and years and years of life. This was not an event for the unimportant; even naïve as I was, I grasped that. And all of them were staring at me.

With a smile, Vladislov wrapped his arm around me and addressed the mob. "My bride's name is Pearl. Be respectful."

Cocked heads, low spoken greetings, far too much interest.

But Vladislov was on to the next thing. Snapping his fingers for a tray of snacks to be delivered by a beautiful woman dressed like a sacrifice for the gods.

Smiling, eyes downcast, she displayed what had been prepared for the humans in attendance as she described the offerings. And that is when I realized there was a clear divide between immortal and mortal.

Some came on the arms of lovers. Most came to serve.

Every last one of them was stunning.

Such as this woman, her neck marked from bites. Her wrists, her arms. Her exposed thighs. "I am of Grecian stock. My line has been fostered by Ivan. O negative, if it suits your taste."

Her plate of food was for the human pets, and her body was for the guests.

And she was happy. I had faced enough smiles serving ungrateful men and women to know the difference.

"Ah, Cassandra. Never could I forget you." He popped a savory bit of deliciousness between my slack lips, taking up the beauty's arm. "I will enjoy this."

Chewing, cheeks puffed from too large a bite, I could not respond. Instead, I watched her moan when my lover pierced her glowing skin.

He sipped.

And I hated seeing it with every fiber of my flawed being.

Before I might stop the hiss, it came from my mouth. Automatic, utterly embarrassed, my hands covered my crimson lips. I knew mortification.

And I worked to justify all of it. Of course he ate. I ate. We all ate.

But I had never seen him partake.

Had I not refused the bath of immortal blood? Yet here I was acting like a monster.

And Vladislov drank deeper.

He drank until the poor girl swooned. Until I put my hand to his bicep and asked him to let her go.

Others came to cart her off, yet her pretty figure was soon replaced. Other immortals taking a sip of the next beauty offered as a snack to the guests.

There was no need to speak of how embarrassed, confused, horrified, enticed I was.

It was so much so that I took a glass of wine from a passing human's tray. He too was dressed as an offering and marked with the wounds of the vampire's trade.

Drinking too fast, I coughed, spilled red wine on a red dress... and knew I was a fool.

"You're charming when you're jealous."

My lip shook as I cut a glance to my right, to my tormentor. In that moment, I saw in him the window I had so desired, so needed, in my past. I saw something worth working for. And I had no idea what to make of myself or these feelings.

My thighs were already smeared in the watery aftermath of our passion. A daughter I did not remember and knew would hate me was soon to arrive. My hair was a mess, my throat itched under the collar, and I was—

Vladislov, snarled. "Why must that boy try me so?"

Boy? I looked up and saw an old man. Sporting a paunch and a threadbare sweater, regularness moved through perfection. Cut through it, more like. The sea parted.

"Erev tov, Father. This must be Pearl."

14

PEARL

The old man smiled in the kind way I'd seen grandfathers smile at children. A calm gesture, a patient one that held wisdom and lacked... fangs. Because I could sense that he was like me, that the sharpness of what set us apart from both human and vampire was a burden. That he worked to embrace his nature yet deny his hunger.

That he understood me. That he felt compassion for a stranger.

Another Daywalker.

I wasn't alone. Such knowledge gave me a profound sense of joy and left me reeling. "You're like me!"

My companion scoffed. "He's nothing like you. The boy is an impudent pain in my ass."

Gesturing at the old man's informal clothing, rude, and clearly annoyed, Vladislov sneered. "What were you thinking arriving in such a state? As Darius was my offspring, and Jade his daughter, you are a clear blood relation. Yet you show up to your queen's wedding dressed like a beggar… wearing that face?"

A face lined by years yet still somehow fresh.

With a peacemaking nod, the stranger replied, "No insult was intended."

Vladislov ground his teeth, leaving the muscles in his jaw jumping. "Your throat is uncovered."

The old man sighed. "As my father is failing to make an introduction, allow me. My given name is Yeshua. It's a pleasure to meet you, Pearl." He held out a hand so I might shake it. The first being at the party aside from Vladislov who dared touch me.

I did not take his hand, not when I could feel how Vladislov seethed. Instead, I offered a polite, "Hello."

Vladislov did not move his body in front of me, but it was as if he intended to shield me all the same. "You were warned never to approach her without permission."

But it was as if the incensed monster at my side had never spoken. The old man's conversation was only for me. "He's written to me about you, countless emails detailing your history. I feel as if I know you."

What?

Outright exasperation was met with equal parts boredom when Vladislov countered, "Countless? You always were one for drama. There have been seventy-eight emails precisely. How many times must I lecture you on the importance of accuracy?"

Though I had denied the old man's hand, he placed his on my shoulder. "It wasn't done to invade your privacy. It was done to document a monumental occurrence. You see, Pearl, the pages recount your life and all the ways in which the consequences of my existence complicated it."

His hand was warm, not the brimstone touch of the beast who held me to his side, arm around my waist, and palm open on my belly. If Vladislov was fire, this man was sunlight.

If Vladislov was beautifully hideous, that old man was painstakingly ordinary.

And I was extremely confused. "I don't understand."

Did the man look embarrassed? It was so hard to tell when his gaze was so deep. "I've been told my father sends you a priest each day for a private mass and confession."

He used to.

I had not seen a holy man since Vladislov had

first penetrated me, nor had I asked for one. In that moment, it dawned on me that I had forgotten. Where was my rosary? Had I forgotten to bring it to a wedding?

Before I fell from the knife edge of nerves into hysterics, Vladislov spoke softly at my ear. "Your rosary is in my pocket, my soul. You may have it in this moment if you wish."

What I wished was to know why the man before me seemed as if he felt grief at the mention of the beads I used to pray. Instead, I took a deep breath and focused on the fact that this was my daughter's wedding and I had already made enough mistakes. "What is an email?"

The old man shook off his gloom, responding with a kind smile. "An electronic letter, typed instead of written by hand. As my father refuses to communicate with me in any other way, we rarely exchange words unless they are in written form. He believes it to be a lesson on the power of truth in the written word over the spoken one. But if you could see the things he's written, you'd understand that he lacks the ability to tell the truth in even the most basic of exchanges. Just because it's been written down does not make it true. Read any newspaper these days and you'll find it's just as easy to lie with the pen as it is with the tongue."

With his free hand, Vladislov physically

removed the old man's touch from my shoulder. "You are not amusing me, child."

For a brief moment, the old man glanced at my companion—an expression of weariness, of deep concern aging his face all the more. "Heaven knows it will be many ages before reconciliation between us is possible, especially after I tell her the truth. But it is good to see you."

Dry laughter preceded Vladislov's threat. "Son, I could end you with a thought. And I'm very *tempted*."

As if they shared a private, dark joke, the old man chuckled. He chuckled as if he was not only fearless, but the more powerful between them. "I am the only thing you ever created that is good. You have no more power to end me than I have the power to end you."

When I had been dragged into Darius' Cathedral, the world moved around me as it did now. I knew the son Vladislov claimed to have fathered. I remembered the dreams where they fought in the desert. But that man was not this man. Just like the angel's form Vladislov had taken was not the monster I knew him to be.

Turning his face from his offspring, Vladislov looked down at me. "You're frightening her."

I did not return the glance. How could I? How could I look away from what might be standing before me? How could I reconcile an immediate and unintentional overflow of love and resentment? "Jesus?"

Brown eyes soft, voice like cool water on burnt skin, Vladislov's son said, "My father will work to convince you that there is no God. It will drive his every move to draw your love from Grace so he might drink it down himself. Do not listen to him. God is in all of us, even in him. God is the love we feel for one another and the forgiveness we strive to extend. Compassion, patience, acceptance, that is the face of God."

Lips came to my ear, but not those of the man speaking to me. They were the same lips that had been all over my body for days on end. "Do you see the flaw in his argument, my soul?" Vladislov stood taller, arm around me as he mocked his offspring. "Boy, it is true a priest was delivered every day to satisfy my bride's indoctrinated need to confess her sins and ask for repentance. You see as clearly as I that she is as innocent as any might be. What sins might she carry? Yet she weeps. Did you hear her prayers? Did the *Father* you prefer to me deliver her? No, son, that figment of your imagination did not. I did. Just as I delivered you."

The old man did not rise to the bait. Instead, he smiled at me, gracious and calm. "It was a pleasure meeting you, Pearl. I hope, in time, we might get to know one another."

Groaning as if this conversation taxed him down to his bones, Vladislov said, "You may stay. But change out of those rags and wear the face I gave you."

It seemed a lighthearted exchange. "I will, Father, if you wear the face God gave you."

The nightmare at my side smiled, his bone-cracking hold on me easing. "And this is where I reply that every face is my face. To which you will say 'Exactly, and they all came from God.' And we will go back and forth for eternity yet get nowhere. How many rocks must I roll away after you've been mauled by the very cattle you seek to *enlighten* before you come to see the world for what it is?"

"I see it clearly, and I worry for those who live in your earthly kingdom." The old man's attention turned to where I clung to Vladislov's arm. "Though, if she really is your soul, there may be hope for all of us yet."

Though he turned to leave, the old man was interrupted by a monster thoroughly up to no good. "One more thing, son. There has been some debate between sweet Pearl and I. Your accidental religion with its myriad rituals has sparked some confusion. So you are best to end the debate. Is she or is she not my wife?"

Everything in the old man's expression seemed to say he had strong thoughts on the matter. "In the Jewish faith to which I was born and to which I adhere, the Zohar claims that a husband and wife are one soul, separated only through their descent to this world. When they are married, they are reunited again. You claim to be reunited. It would follow that she is your wife. No one who has seen my father and still became of one flesh with such a beast could be anything but wife."

I might have had wine spilt on my dress. My hair might have been embarrassingly mussed. I might have been uneducated and naive. But at no time in my years had I not recognized an insult. "Excuse me?"

Vladislov's fingers on my belly fluttered one by one, as if delighted. "She's offended, but she doesn't know why. How charming."

I was offended. I was baffled. And I was being discussed as if I were a sheep and they were wolf and shepherd. All because I could not find the words to ask what my brain clamored to know. Was this real? Was this some trick? Was I speaking with Jesus? How did he only know me from the thing called email? Why must I perpetually be the butt of some joke? Why had God forsaken me? Why had Darius been allowed to toy with me? Of all the saviors that might have come to save the sinner, why had it been Vladislov who carried me out of the dark?

As if he could see straight down to my soul, as if he could pick through the mess of my thoughts, the old man said, "God makes us what we are, tempers the great by terrible trials. Had your life been anything other than it was, I could not hope that you are indeed my father's soul. Which is why I fear that if you will not take him as your husband, this world will be doomed before all those living in it have a chance to find the peace of God."

First, there was a vicious chuckle. Then, Vladislov smacked his lips. He smacked his lips and then bent me back over his arm, thrusting his tongue into my mouth in a salacious kiss that stole my air. He even dared tear into my bodice to clutch a breast as if he intended to fuck me right there in the middle of the crowd. It wasn't until I was breathless from fighting and dared bite him that he drew back, laughing as if the world were wonderful and my flustered state truly divine.

Jesus was gone. The party moved around us as if nothing untoward had taken place.

And I? I looked back at a monster who mouthed the word "wife" before he pulled together my dress.

It was then I saw her. The bride dressed in white, who unlike the rest of the crowd seemed to be paying close attention to whatever had just passed. Our eyes met. Mine blue, hers glowing red.

She sneered.

And I loved her for it.

I loved her as if she'd always been mine.

15

PEARL

Over the course of my years, and especially of late, I imagined many things—about my future, about a world I longed for yet retreated from... about my unknown child. Thoughts of her unsettled me the most.

My baby could have been anything, grand or monstrous. One look at her might have cut out my heart for a multitude of reasons that made me unworthy of such a gift. Not once in my life had I ever considered that I'd birth a child. I was cursed. I was sickly. Yet I had. Not that I remembered it, or her, or why, or how, or anything. I'd even tried to, finding only a black hole in my thoughts. And that hole was far too easy to fall into and so much more difficult to climb free of.

Entire pieces of my brain had just been yanked out and filled up with sawdust.

The few memories of Darius I had were enough. Never did I want to know the rest. But I burned with something deeper than anger, a constant pinprick behind my eyes.

An infant's creation, her time in my body, her birth had been torn out of my mind. A person I was entirely blind to, who I would have never known existed had Vladislov not told me she walked the earth, had no idea I was her mother.

A disturbing, worrying, guilt-inducing horror I'd have to answer to God for. At the feet of my Lord, I'd have to explain my misgivings and disgust. I'd have to confess that the first mention of her did not bring me joy. It brought me horror.

I'd have to ask forgiveness for the sin of bitterness-laced fascination. That I wasn't at her wedding for her benefit, but for purely selfish longing to know *who I was*.

A sick curiosity wrapped up in pretend obligation to a fully grown woman.

Yet, one look at the woman my baby had become... and every last pang of disgust and uncertainty blew from my skin like unsettled dust when a tomb was disturbed.

I grew lighter. I knew that somewhere stuck in

the untouchable parts of my memory, I had felt that child move inside me and loved her.

Had her first cries been beautiful? Had she nursed from my breast after I delivered her into the world?

I bet her head had smelled divine.

What had she looked like as a baby?

"You want to know, so I will tell you this." Softly at my ear, a creature who could see into my darkness whispered, "True to form, he cut her out when your condition became inconvenient. Though you fought him despite your entrails spilling everywhere, Darius never allowed you the honor of holding her in your arms. Not after she'd drawn your attention away from him once too often. The squalling, naked, and bloody babe was delivered to the man Jade will wed tonight. You were never allowed to love her."

But I did love her. Right in that moment, I loved her as I have never loved anything. And it moved me to cuddle closer to the beast whispering ugly secrets in my ear—to lean on him as if there was nothing more natural than sharing the moment my heart felt whole for the first time in all my existence.

As a bride, my baby was a vision.

Perfect in every conceivable way in my eyes. Even the obvious evil of her.

That was how God had designed her, and God was flawless.

The arm around me grew all the more reassuring. "And if you follow that logic, then you must also concede that you are perfect. I'll even concede that this might be the only topic upon which your false God and I agree."

God loves his children just as they are. God is love. The immeasurable love I had for my child was the love God had for all things. Even Vladislov.

Even Darius.

Who had harmed my child by taking her from me.

A thought that led to a complicated resentment it was not the time to indulge in. My eyes, my devotion, were for one being only that night.

Jade, her limbs draped in exquisite white lace as she observed me in return.

I knew that high forehead, the more feminine lines of a jaw from my worst nightmares. The aristocratic nose. She was her father made female.

The vivid red of her lips oddly highlighted eyes that burned of hellfire.

There was nothing in that regal woman that had the look of me.

"You're wrong. Her eyes, my soul. They *were* the same shade as yours." Pulling me before his body so I might rest against his chest and enjoy a better view, Vladislov wrapped me tight in his embrace, causing the woman to cock a sculpted dark eyebrow. "Blue as the burning core of the hottest flame. When the day comes for you to know one another, she will find comfort in recognizing that part of herself in you."

I'd never thought much of my eyes, but I would every day from that night forward. I would look in the mirror and see this child, even if that was all of me she had.

"There are portraits of her from when she was younger. I will have one brought to you before sunrise." I could hear the smile in his voice. "You'll see much more of yourself, all the softness. She hides it now with her paint and sharp tongue, because she believed her humanity a weakness. But you are very much a part of her. As Jade grows in confidence as a queen, she will let go of the idea of being only part of herself and embrace the whole."

Watching me, Jade unconsciously touched elegant fingertips to a ruby encrusted contraption circling her throat. It was similar to mine in the sense that it covered from jaw to collarbone, but far less delicate than the collar around my neck.

Even from a distance, I could tell it made her uncomfortable. That it must chafe and be difficult to move in. Edges of it even appeared sharp, a constant scratch against delicate skin.

Leaning farther into my personal demon's warm embrace, I whispered, "You said her throat would be bare."

I felt him smell my hair, nuzzling into me intimately no matter who darted startled looks in our direction. Positively sentimental, he cooed, "Isn't it romantic? Malcom won't let her take it off, though it clings and annoys. He wants his love to know he's always there and she's always his."

I didn't like that one bit.

"She fights it, believes she hates it. But she's lying to herself. That girl needs the reminder as much as she needs his rule. Jade might be Queen of the Americas, but he is her custodian. And I swear to you, all life on the planet is safer for it. Your daughter is a right bitch when she's in a temper."

Hissing under my breath, I dared break the spell of observation and cut a glance back to the man who insulted my daughter. "Don't say that about her!"

Vladislov chuckled. "She has your fire too. I doubt you realize how fierce you can be. Not one in a billion would dare speak to me as you do. Not even Darius had the balls. That makes you better than him."

I had never been fierce a day in my life. Women were intended to be meek. Which led to the oddest feeling that I had just been insulted.

Which, of course he knew. He even laughed.

"You pretend to be meek, because that is what you believed was expected of you. But you've ripped out more than one throat in your lifetime—you just have to be pushed far enough to snap. You fought your tormentor for your baby. And you're here, in the midst of the most powerful of our kind, staring down a woman who dislikes your presence... because you are her mother and you have every right to do so."

I began to tune out Vladislov's latest soliloquy just as I would tune out my patrons when I walked from table to table offering cigarettes. In that moment, it didn't matter what he thought. All that mattered was my girl.

Who had caught herself touching the collar and pulled her hand away as if mildly embarrassed. Until a man with hair as bright as hers was dark approached and took her in his arms.

"Malcom. You can say his name."

She glowed, leaned into him, forgot about me entirely.

"Jade is an absolute fool for that boy."

Malcom. That boy. Very normal terms for the veritable angel who had beaten me against a brick wall all those years ago, breaking my jaw as he ripped out my fangs. I could still hear him laughing as I wept, that memory more real to me than the horror I imagined Jade's birth to be.

"Shhhh, don't tremble, Pearl." Warmth stroked over my arms, a deep male voice offering comfort. "He is forbidden from so much as glancing in your direction. And rightly concerned that I might change my mind about his continued existence."

My Jade so clearly adored him that should Vladislov dare to harm a pale hair on Malcom's head, I'd be very upset.

Vladislov didn't even try to conceal his irritation. "I know, which is what makes this so unfair to me. How am I supposed to relax when I really want to do unspeakable things but can't because it will upset you? Pity me."

"You're being ridiculous." And oddly cute with the whining. Whining that worked its magic and left me smirking instead of afraid.

Like an eager puppy, Vladislov curled around me. "I promise to behave if you'll give me one kiss."

One kiss, quickly given before he might try to distract me further or delve his hands back into my dress.

Even with the complete lunacy of the situation, it was as if a spark snapped when our mouths met. Chaste yet lingering. When it ended, Vladislov looked down at me, eyes glowing, a soft smile on his lip. "Now, shush. It's beginning."

My daughter and the man who had delivered to

a demon for torment because I had broken an unknown law joined hands.

Beautiful side by side, Jade caught up in her husband's eyes. Even the fool I was could see plain as night that nothing existed to her in that moment but him.

If she loved him, so would I.

Behind me, Vladislov muttered, "Ugh, you're far too gracious."

"I forgive him." And it was really that simple.

Malcom, as if he heard our whisperings, let out a pent-up breath. I don't know why I sensed it, but I felt in that moment that he wanted to glance my way, just for a second. Just to acknowledge what seemed like a gift.

"It *was* a gift. His entire bloodline was at stake should you have refused. I had only granted him five years with Jade before the culling might begin. Now I'm in the mood to reconsider."

Lately, it had become simple to forget just who I was with. An ease had grown between us, even laughter. Passion that seemed to rewrite the very fabric I'd been cut from.

It would just slip my mind in tiny moments.

"Five years was generous and only granted because he led me to where Darius had hidden you away. Had I found the memory in his head, had he tried to hide it, an eternity in a tomb was only the beginning of what he might have suffered. But he came to me, he *knew* there was something vital in so small a memory. He knew, because Darius ripped out his heart, so Jade ripped out the heart of her father and put it in the chest of the man she loves. Darius lives in him in a significant way, so rethink your easy forgiveness in a sentimental moment."

"No. And you cannot tempt me from my decision either, demon."

"Fine." A brisk, irritated *fine*.

"And you will allow him to look at me, and speak to me."

From annoyance to amusement, a snap in temperament from one to the other that kept me on my toes and him *interesting*. "And here you thought to pretend you were meek."

16

VLADISLOV

My will poured over the gathered guests at the wedding party in such a way that Pearl was clueless as to my designs. I deigned who might hear us, who might so much as see her. Each glance she garnered was at my whim for a specific purpose. Whether it was to announce to other females with whom I had shared physical pleasure not to think to proposition me for more. Or to dash the hopes of those who clung to the idea that someday I might return their ardent affection. Or to ordain that this is your goddess and I am her slave. Or so males might know just what would become of them should they brush against her or think to tempt her from me.

And they would. That was the game amongst

our kind. They didn't know I wore a plain face for a purpose. I didn't flaunt my riches. Why should I? Their riches were my riches. The very blood in their veins, regardless of their sire, came from me.

I knew what I had created the first time I was tempted to set my vein to the mouth of a near-dead mortal. It was as if the world had unfolded before me. A scroll accounting family trees, impossibilities, eternity, joy, sorrow, fascination to end my loneliness and agitation at how difficult my children would be.

Those first vampires, my bright-eyed babies, were all dead.

I ended them, one by one, after they had left my flock and begun flocks of their own. Their purpose had been served—propagation. Their egos, titles, the worship of them in temples... it was too much and far too gaudy.

Never did I request temples to my name or call for minions to hear my gospel. Not that temples didn't exist. And it would be an outright lie to claim that several of my names were not called out in vain by those foolish enough to think I might give them power. But unlike my son and his faulty religion, I had been born a living god to my people and understood exactly the flaws with such a path.

Worship led to tragedies like my poor Pearl, her

hammering heart, the way she clutched at the rosary I slipped into her fingers—one she didn't even realize she held.

I would be picking apart that knot in her life for eons. On the day when Pearl's eyes truly opened to the way of the world, she would be…

Inconsolable.

My poor darling. Maybe it was a kindness that my son had filled her head with false ideals. The longer she held to some sort of faith, the more time she would have to see that all along it truly had been *I* fulfilling her needs.

Heart already breaking for her, I pressed a kiss to her hair. She really did smell of sunshine, of goodness. She smelled of all the things that had been torn away from me the day fate dared try to take my soul from me.

Humming in her hair, I confessed an open truth. "I love you."

No change came to her bearing, no stiffness. No fear in her scent.

Progress!

Tenderly swaying as if the pair of us moved to music that was ours and ours alone, I enjoyed this corner of my mind while the rest of me worked.

As I said, I exerted my will on all who stood in attendance.

I whispered in the minds of every last immortal. A cohesive symphony of soft, indomitable rule. A smattering could hear it, the thousand voices moving like mist over thought, or like daggers through resistance. Some could only feel it, taking comfort or distress.

This is mine.

Do not touch.

Look at her and envy.

Look at her and know she can unknowingly decide your fate with little more than a frown.

Look at her and love her.

Look at how I touch her, how I hold her. I would never touch you in such a way.

Look at how she trusts me, how she fits against my body because we are one.

Do you see her mouth? There was no need for paint. Her lips are red from my attention.

Do you smell her cunt? My seed even now drips down her thigh.

I will make her fat with life as she drinks down yours.

Never question me.

Offend her and it won't only be you I unravel thread by thread. I will eat your home, your children, your children's children. You will be erased from the world.

Weep if you wish, but I will never love you.

Prostrate at her feet. Offer your wrists.

Those who bleed the most shall gain my favor. Those who seek to deny my soul her due shall learn the true meaning of regret.

Yes, I had a flair for drama.

True, few in that myriad collection knew just what I *might* be to them.

Rumors of the winged-demon had begun to spread in private whispers between those I wished to suspect.

Those who did not deserve to know me? I plucked the thought straight from their puny brains.

Yet, it should be noted that when working with immortal minds, it takes something more than a soft spoken order to gain the attention of something that has already seen everything and found it wanting.

Those with the skill and the years whispered back to me, carrying on their current conversations as if we were not discussing the very fabric of their existence.

"No insult is intended toward your bride. What excellent taste you have. I've longed for a Daywalker of my own."

Then fuck a human and make your own.

"It's been ages, Vladislov. How do you fair?

Oh, I am well. I am well enough that the world

might actually bloom for a space. Well, maybe after one more plague.

"Gifts will be sent."

Indeed they would be. The most honored of the flocks would be bled for my soul's breakfast. And it would be delivered, steaming hot, in jeweled cups. There would be gowns, art, trinkets, land, palaces, secrets....

And those who delivered most would have no true understanding of why they did as they did. Something deep within would niggle at them to produce, that their survival was on the line.

All of this would be kept from Pearl. Well, not the blood. She deserved to sample the fare. But all the chalices, all the wealth, would be tucked away. She would drink from the same crystal to which she had grown accustomed. Live in what she considered quite lavish circumstances, though they were far from what true depravity might offer.

The simple things made her soul sing all the louder.

Caskets of jewels? Those could wait and be playthings for our children. An entire museum of cups crafted just for her lips would be erected in some far off country. To amuse her, I'd take her there some day.

She would laugh to see it.

Gold, diamonds, silver... cups carved from

meteors. I could already say for certain that she would still prefer the simple cut crystal.

But few would know such secrets.

Of course, there would be grand soirees in which she might hold a finer cup. But the guest list would be excruciatingly hand-selected. Maya could be trusted with such a task, should I be able to tempt her away from her immediate hunt of those who dared plunder her homelands for what humans considered ancient—such a laughable term— artworks of one of the most interesting and valuable cultures. Nok, they called it these days.

She'd been a wonder, born to a family of wonders.

Such a soft spot I had for wonders. Most of whom were wise enough to take the invitation in my less *structured* flock.

Ach, but Maya was also in love with a human man, which I pointedly ignored and equally found intriguing. She lived with him as a human.

"Work from home."

What a term, what a marvelous construct. Vampires anywhere smart enough to install the proper windows could play human. She had children!

Hid their nutritional *needs* in their food.

That would be an epic disaster the day she came clean that she was older than dirt, wanted in several countries for very grisly murders of art "collectors," and that they would not age past their prime.

The husband… would she change him?

Not that I cared. Really. I didn't. I even wondered if she did it all to amuse me. *That's how self-centered I am.* Am I not a wonder on my own?

She, who fought for the treasures of a people long lost, had seen me in my hideous glory thanks to Pearl's request I show her my true face. And Maya had wanted to know when she too might have such wings.

Adorable.

Unlike the stunning brunette of true Grecian stock daring to glare at me, and who I would unmake before sunrise. One pretty female I had turned thousands of years ago.

She'd had her time in the shadow of my interest.

And she knew better than to allow jealousy and dark thoughts of comparison between herself and my *true* bride. Apphia seethed, demanding her due for servicing me for so long to be thrown over for a skinny daywalker with a mind she could easily see was Swiss cheese.

That's how she thought of it! How *dare* she!

She even dared ask me if I had fallen into madness.

As I stood in the midst of the strongest I had created, as the most powerful of my kind fluttered and gathered like bees about their queen. As my dear bride laid her eyes upon her child for the first time and worked through the complications that arose from such a monumental occasion, I tore the jealous harlot's mind to ribbons.

But with subtlety. After all, this was a wedding, and it would be inappropriate to make a scene.

First, I took away her name, so that she would never recall it. A small thing that would lead to very amusing situations later. A thing she wouldn't notice, not while she was still arguing with me over the sacrifices she made for me. Not when she dared claim that she loved me in a way my Pearl could not.

Nothing, ever, would love me as my soul already did. Pearl wasn't aware of her connection yet, how woven together we'd already become. My son was right in claiming that any who saw my true face and willingly took me into their body in that state and survived the onslaught had to be my equal.

There was a reason I called her my soul. But Pearl was so much more.

If I was a demon, she was an angel.

Maybe in ten thousand years she'd have white, feathered wings and glow with the sunlight running through her veins. Instead of the imps she had imagined, our babies could be fat cherubs.

Wouldn't that be cute?

The creature in my arms spoke, her attention fixed on the couple preparing to link their immortality together. "Vlad, you're growling."

Fine. I was.

Wait? Had she just called me Vlad?

SHE HAD!

I was now Vlad!

A pet name. A term of endearment.

How my heart soared!

Fuck Apphia. Not literally. Eww. Never again.

So what if I had seen that girl's beauty while I awaited the return of my soul? Yes, I had taken the maiden from her family. Sure, we had eaten her parents once she'd woken to the night and made sport of her siblings until any remnant of her human line had ended so her vampire line might begin.

But Apphia had never borne me a child—all the seed sprayed meant for another and dumped because time was monotonous and pricks liked to leak into slits.

I owed her nothing. Not after the palaces, the notoriety, the power, and the distinction she held with our race. Foolish woman.

Who would I make the new queen of the European nations? Maya?

No.

Maya would laugh at the very idea. She was

already a queen and needed no nations to prove that point.

Vacuums in power were extremely annoying. "You have no idea how hard it is to get anyone to do their job these days, my love. Really. Can I have another kiss? Please?"

Ah! I had made Pearl laugh. She found my angst amusing, did she? Well, that I could lay on thick. "One kiss, sweet soul. I promise to keep my hands out of your bodice. And yes, I know you are blushing and still embarrassed. But those tits. Come now, darling. They are perfect, and I am incapable of resisting."

She giggled even more. Giggled! Oh, I was so getting laid later. "If I kiss you again, will you please be quiet?"

"Yes." *No*.

Another quick slant of her lips upon mine, her neck craning to meet me.

I felt the erections rise from those males who found pleasure in females, all of whom I had called to look. Showing off my bride...

...was gauche.

But really. If they were not allowed to touch, they should at least suffer knowing why. Pearl was stunning. Her pulse beat at her throat as if she were human.

She exuded the scent of all things delectable, I could gobble her up.

I would have had she been born nearer to my turning.

Oh.

Well then.

Now I knew why she had taken so long to be reborn. I lacked any sort of self-control when it came to such a being. I would have killed her on accident and wept over her bones until the earth rotted.

And it would have rotted. That was how it worked.

All in me reflected, as it should. This was my kingdom.

And her new name? Pearl.

How had I not seen?

A bit of sand in the belly of an oyster. Rolled about. Made smooth. Made precious and glorious over ages.

I cackled, startling my bride. Head thrown back, I practically howled at the moon.

A pearl. *A Pearl*. The scratching bit of sand in the world—my realm's—belly. Because I refused to let her leave me and she had sworn on the life of her newly born monster to return. And here she was reborn and named and hilariously exact.

Nothing had ever been so hysterically deserved. Oh, fuck you, fates.

Now I could stand near so much deliciousness and not crunch her bones in my maw.

Enough pretending. With just a bit of effort, I could make others see whatever I wished. Fabric tore as my body expanded. Wings knocked into spectators who had no clue why they sidestepped or what had sent their hair flying back.

My precious Pearl liked me as I was.

So I *was*.

But only for her eyes.

Everyone else saw what I told them to see, including the couple preparing to speak their vows. No soul knew me but her.

She didn't even mind that I singed her dress.

Looking back and forth, her concern not for her skin that burned or the way I dug my claws in until just a touch of her blood scented the air, Pearl asked, "Why isn't anyone screaming?"

Of course she would be more concerned for strangers than herself.

"Because I am yours and they cannot see me. Because you love me and they don't." Spittle dripped from my fang, hissing when it landed on red silk.

One time, she rubbed her lips together, turning in my arms to look over the burning mess of my fine clothes. "I really want to watch my daughter get married. Can you please control yourself until it's over?"

"Yes." And that was truth. Every last winsome part of me settled. Physically, I formed around her, wings and all. I took her in my embrace, as I was, as she was.

The ceremony began.

17

VLADISLOV

How long had it been since I actually paid any attention to such tripe? Modern weddings. I must have attended several. After all, I knew the dress code and the expectations. But gatherings were a question of impression—of the mental variety in my case.

All talk in my head ceased.

My damned offspring's blood-born Daywalker child linked hands with a man whose easy breaths were the wedding gift of my wife. The mother of the bride.

My wife, who had borne that child in pain so excruciating that I would indeed scrap that memory from her mind, even if she hated me for it later. Never would Pearl see what had been done or know how much of her was lost that day.

My Pearl and that Pearl were not and never would be the same.

Jade had been granted what Darius had stolen from my soul. It glittered under her skin for those who knew how to look. The shimmer of a Pearl. It made her.

As strange as such a thing was to say, *it made her*.

Her mother's loss, the fight, the abundant will to save her child… the universe had passed that to Jade.

Who glowed.

Who was truly at peace so long as Malcom was near.

I knew exactly how she felt.

"I give myself to you while I take everything that you are." Spoken in Malcom's native tongue. Words I translated, in soft hues of speech so Pearl might know what took place.

She shivered under the burn of my wings.

"A world I lay at your feet."

Jade did not know the language in which her bridegroom spoke, but she knew every last promise made by the River Seine. Just as Pearl knew me and would soon recognize what we were.

"Eternity by my side. For eternity, I shall care for you."

Jade, as queen, would not return the vows before

guests. That would be something done in private, out of the ears of the immortals she ruled. Still, she spilled tears of happiness.

Clear as night, I could see the dark things stuck inside her falling away like dead flies off a reborn corpse. Jade was made new.

"She looks so happy."

My darling one was desperate that her words sang true. So I let her see. I opened up just enough for her to see what I saw.

Jade was in bliss.

Malcom loved her as no man ever had loved, save I.

Weeping in joy, my bride made demands. "You can't ever hurt him. Never."

"As you wish."

Blubbering, extremely cute, and every bit the embarrassing mother at a wedding, Pearl added, "Men don't... they don't think of women as he thinks of her. He sees beyond her beauty or what she can do for him."

Black talon tracing her cheek, I said, "Come now. I love you even beyond the ways in which he loves her. And you know that."

"But *you* are not a man." As if that might make her not realize her slip.

The very slip that brought a frightening grin to my lips. Sharp teeth on display, I let a black forked tongue trace my lips. "You know I love you."

She wouldn't lie. She wasn't capable of it. That didn't mean she wasn't going to be shy. "I know you think you do."

Taking her chin, I turned her back to the spectacle. To Jade and Malcolm.

He offered his naked throat to his queen.

As she nuzzled in, he found the place where her collar split just enough, where fangs placed with infinite care could be snapped off by the prey, daring enough to try to drink from such a guarded throat.

He pierced her flesh delicately. She tore at his—an expected statement, considering their vastly different stations. And they fed.

The sucking sounds were suggestive to an extreme, inspiring the onlookers to begin their own feast, whether with lovers or upon those humans delivered as snacks.

One moment, the couple was feasting on one another. The next, Malcom manhandled his queen into his arms.

They vanished into the night.

After her daughter was gone, as Pearl processed, it was the first time I had ever heard regret in my bride's mind for her shortened fangs. Imagination full of her own potential wedding, she knew there was no skin she might break.

"I would slit my throat before every last one of my chattel. You could drink me to death." Every word sang through my being.

She turned in my arms yet kept her eyes on where the ribbons of my shirt still smoked. "Don't be silly."

The tip of my thumb delved into her mouth, the world blocked out so none might see or hear. Wings raised so even the sky had no access to my female, I pressed the pad of that thumb to her sad fang. "They will grow back. Until then, cut me to ribbons in any way you please."

Shy blue eyes went from cracked, fiery chest to my hideous face. "This has been the strangest night of my life."

All that, spoken around the digit that still teased at her slight fang. That pressed until my skin gave the flavor of her favorite treat.

Not that my delicate flower would suck me before the crowd.

Kidding. She was already licking at the droplet. The poor dear had absolutely no control once she had a taste of me.

Who would blame her? I was hideously delectable.

"I'm going to fuck you here. On this ground.

Where everyone will see it," I told her as her pupils blew on the high of a God's blood. "And you will be angry with me for it later."

"No."

"But my hand is already up your skirt." And it was. A very human-looking hand attached to a very human-looking body. That had a human-looking cock that she already fingered, unaware that she was addicted.

Everyone fell into states of undress.

Pearl's first orgy.

I let her keep her ripped crimson dress, working myself in after her back hit the planks of the platform created for the wedding.

One thrust saw me deep in my bride's body before she might recognize the depravities I pulled her down to.

Blood-red satin singed and bundled to her waist, I thrust like a king might into a serving wench he favored. The girl was shocked. The girl's mind trying to catch up as things took place beyond her ken.

Pearl keened, cunt weeping about my human girth.

The cry was not for my tricks. It was for my falseness. This was not my cock. This was not my body. But I made a show for all to see. Her perfect tits bounced from the tears in her bodice I had prepared for just this moment.

At no time did she fight back. Instead, she tilted her hips so it might end all the sooner and she might die of shame in private.

Rough, because she needed rough as the moans, hisses, and screams of pain rose up on that platform, I took her chin and forced.

My Pearl liked to be forced.

A dark secret I had manipulated to my advantage. "We celebrate."

A tear escaped the corner of her eye.

"They have to see me this way, my soul. They have to watch me ride you as if I was one of them." I was so close to spilling, just to end this. "I will fuck you into the next century day and night, while you feed on me until I am sad skin on old bones. Cry harder. I will finish sooner. And they who do not know me will see and respect the claiming."

Not waiting for a reply, I caught a peaked, red nipple with the flick of the tongue and a trick of the teeth. And I made her writhe.

Dancing as the ripples and waves rocked her on my invasive, hideous human cock, I made the show one worth remembering.

Of course, I added in some flair my bride would have never abided.

I came. She gaped.

I had given her no climax even as her womb was assaulted with my spend.

Which drove doubt hard on the heels of a maiden's stained morality.

Resting my forehead against hers, I whispered, "This was for show in honor of a wedding. Expected. It's easier to rip off the band-aid."

Her teeth went to my throat, because my words offended her to such a degree. It was utter reflex. Cornered prey fighting back... as she had done so many times. Yet fangless, she could do nothing.

I could do everything.

I could see all the men who had used her in this way. Noted their faces, their names, and made easy decisions on how to shuck their descendants into feeding pens. Bending the rules, I also empowered her in those memories, ripping the inborn church guilt away from a creature doing nothing more than trying to defend itself and succeeding.

The flesh on my neck parted, because I willed it to do so, and black blood more delightful than sin drenched the tongue of an angry woman.

She drank me, that sad human cock inside her, until her belly poked out. Falling back and panting with fullness.

This moment, she would not understand for some time. But it was the price she had to pay to see Jade wed.

For standing with me as wife in public.

For my love.

"Did I hurt you?"

Glassy-eyed, she stared at the stars, utterly ignoring my presence.

"If I had made you like it, that would have been wrong." Why was I begging her to understand what had been on the agenda before time had been written? *"This is not me."*

Cerulean eyes moved from vacancy to daggers. "And that is what makes it so horrid."

My monstrous cock changed before the rest of me might stop it. Groaning in discomfort from the stretch, my bride's hips wriggled to make room even as her body tried to remove me. "You refused the bath. You were ashamed of your breasts and how I enjoyed you. I knew public fucking would unnerve you, but your survival and acceptance require you to bend at least *once* to your heritage. I can make you forget this."

Not that I would.

Drunk on my blood, she struck out with the tiniest, cutest little moon-white claws. My cheek was torn to shreds.

Really.

Down to the teeth and gums.

Another dollop of come burst forth unexpectedly for us both.

This must have been what the idea of heaven had been formed of.

"Do it again," I begged. "Rip me to ribbons down to the bone."

"No." The weight of words she had never been able to speak in the past fell on me like boulders. "Get out of my body."

Hips snapping back, I pulled out the recrafted, human dick as if it had been burned with acid.

And then she vanished.

My bride left me there at her own daughter's wedding.

Shucking the fluids from my cock, I buttoned up the tatters of my demon-torn clothing, certain I was in more trouble than I anticipated. And that she should not tempt me with a chase.

Pearl had no idea how much I craved a hunt. But for the first time since the sky lost its stars at night thanks to the cities' ambient light, I felt a twinge of fear.

She could be anywhere. And precious as they were, despite the time required to craft them, Pearls were delicate.

18

PEARL

I should have known. This is where all men, *or monsters*, left things. With their seed inside me and my pride crushed. Yet this time, I had taken my innate foolishness past the pale. I had *appreciated* the monster. Not because he called me pretty or had given my pretty things. Because he had seemed to listen. I thought it was *me* he saw.

Not my tits.

Not my face.

Not the things I might do with my mouth or the way the place between my legs might sate him.

And though it had only been a blip of time, considering... considering the decades it had taken me to walk from California to the East Coast. It had been, what? A month? Maybe three?

Half a year?

Ten years?

Who could tell how time passed when most of it was spent lost in the huge black hole of my mind?

He had seemed so hideously kind. Ugly, grotesque in his mercy poured on my wounds. Care.

For a *thing* like me.

And ultimately, he had been no different from any other man who had pushed me down and thrust in.

No different than the demon who had kept me for a pet in a stone box. I was still a pet, just with better surroundings.

The rosary in my grip, I could feel the beads begin to crack from the force at which I fisted it. "I bet you're laughing at me, aren't you?"

Of course he was.

How could a crispy head on a pike do anything but?

In France, I had been standing in the deep of night. Now, moments later, I was dumped in a pile on the soft grass of a balmy garden at dusk. Back in Manhattan where I'd once been so sure all my dreams might come true. Where I'd had a window.

The sun set at my back, warming my skin, leaving my shadow stretching over the drooping eyelids of a grotesque familiarity.

It didn't matter if I was in France, or my golden

city, or walking dusty roads, or begging strangers for scraps. I had been born in hell.

I had never left hell.

And hell would never leave me.

I, the damned, whose slit ached with unsatiated need, sloppy with spend. A backward body buzzing with irritation at having not reached climax while totally unaroused by the horror before me.

Darius.

The pike jammed into the stump of his neck was layered with what seemed to be an endlessly dripping crust. The head *juicy*, despite its scabbed and hideous burns.

What should have been shrunken from the rigors of the sun and starvation still possessed form. Cheekbones, sharp but identifiable. Burnt hair leaning toward the deepest brown. Lips.

I knew the sting of those lips.

The sun fully set, drooping eyelids twitched.

"Yes. You *are* laughing."

So loud it almost felt as if my ears bled.

"I know this place." Turning, humidity leaving torn, red silk to stick to my skin, I took in the jutting stone edifice that seemed to erupt from the ground itself. A cathedral. A cloister. A monastery. A place where screams had seeped into the stone.

My screams so small in the cacophony.

I was *home*.

How I knew that—considering not once before that night could I recall my eyes setting upon the outside of the terrifying warren—was utterly beyond me. But I knew. This was where I had rotted. This was where I had begged God to redeem me.

This was where I had sold my soul.

There was very little I could pull on from my memory, but I remembered the abject pain, how it was twisted up inside me as if it were pleasure, and how the little of me left splintered and let evil in just to make it stop.

Lying in my own blood and shit, I had begged. *I had begged.*

The ground had shaken.

Darius had left me.

And here he must have been since. Head on a pike in a garden outside his usurped kingdom now controlled by the child we'd created.

While I wandered a room, frightened and alone.

While I uncovered the secrets of my tomb. A Coney Island funhouse of horrors written in my own hand. Beautiful things too. Paintings, jewels, indecent nightwear. Tiny forgotten flecks of blood on the stone.

In that room, before I had extinguished the last candle, I found myself.

And found that I was nothing of worth.

Forgotten.

There would never be salvation. So I had sang the same songs I had heard mothers sing to their young as I journeyed from place to place.

And I had dreamed of nothing.

Yet still sang.

Though my bones were brittle and my mind was rotted into mush, I heard another pick up the fading tune.

Hideous life dripped down a withered, resisting throat.

That first hacking cough, trying to expel not only the music but succor.

I fought each part of me as it came slowly back to life. I could not take a single further second of *myself*.

All of it had been….

I knew the bible back and forth, and no scripture burned into what was left of my mind might assuage whatever I was. My very life was a cancer on the world, one that grew roots into it as I'd desiccated.

The little hairs from those roots, I still felt them tugging me into the ground. Or maybe they were tugging me *back* into the ground.

I had no idea how I had even appeared in this place, in a heap of skirts and weeping. One moment, I looked into the eyes of a monster I had mistakenly trusted. The next, those fuzzy roots—those spreading incessant roots—snapped me back where they had grown.

Home.

That is what I had longed for.

And this.

THIS!!

This godforsaken ground was my home.

Darius rotting on a stick. But alive and hungry—the eyes in his ragged head glowing as he drank me down under the rot of drooping lids.

What was left of him was famished.

Slack jawed head twitching.

Even so, Darius began to heal before my eyes as if such a state could be made beautiful. His eyes, those terrible eyes, looking right at me as if to say that, *yes, he laughed.*

Not that he didn't also beg.

"Come to me, treasure."

Damaged as he was, despite blaring, continuous pain, the demon was dangerous.

And so familiar in the way he picked at my thoughts, indelicately scratching at each memory he fingered through.

I should have gone screaming into the night.

I should have done anything other than meet his eyes and *feel*.

All my pain.

ALL MY PAIN.

Wrapped in a pretty bow of desecration and disappointment.

That thing on the stick hated Vlad. Burned with the blackest bubbling oil of greasy animosity.

I might have hated Vladislov in that moment too, but I hated Darius far more. "I enjoyed lying with him in a way you could never inspire me to enjoy you."

What was I saying? Never had I heard that level of spite in my voice. That dark seed only grew, expanding in my chest until I felt my sad fangs attempt to descend only to ache with the inability to be little more than nubs.

As if that sorry head thought to console me, it whispered in my mind, *"Dear treasure."*

"I'm not your treasure."

"Always. None, but I care for you. Think of what you are now because of me and the sacrifices I made in your name."

Soft grass under my bare feet. Where had my shoes gone? Lost when Vlad pushed me to the planks. Fallen off when I popped out of thin air a few feet too high above the ground and thudded into the earth like a bird shot out of the sky.

Dress torn, wrinkled, sodden, stinking of what had made me seek *home*. Ugly inside and out. So many gemstones around my throat that it ached.

Breath confined, heart racing, I stood as I was. As who I was.

A broken thing.

"Your lips, Pearl. Put them to mine."

"No." Resolute, that filthy word twisted my tongue into the most unfeminine of replies.

I had been designed to be meek. Otherwise, God would not love me. I had allowed males to do horrible things to me in the name of subservience.

And in that moment, held by the heat of blood-red eyes, I swore to myself that it would never happen again. "This sight comforts me, knowing you are trapped on a stick in *my* sun, boiling at midday and begging for scraps at midnight."

"Come, pet." That fiddling in my thoughts, that itch. *"Embrace me. I can save you from them."*

Not that I had not noticed the growing shadows once the sun was no longer a concern, the Cathedral's inhabitants began to gather and whisper, edging nearer where I stood in a breathtaking garden.

The denizens of the Cathedral had seen me. No sun lingered to keep them away. And I was unwelcome.

Openly threatened yet perfectly stalked.

They wished for me to run.

They thirsted for a chase.

Yet still I stood hissing to the head of my

personal demon as it oozed feted matter down the pike. Damn the whispering shadows back to their hell! I had words to say to this beast.

"You tore my baby out of my body!"

And it had words to say to me as well, the tone having skirted from seduction to cruel laughter. *"More than one."*

Bile in the back of my throat, visibly swallowing, I felt the distortion and the fact. "You're lying."

If thoughts could smile, Darius was grinning like he'd eaten my babies for sport. *"I can take you to them. How they cry for their mommy."*

The mental flash of the monster tearing at the flesh of a newborn was jammed into my brain like a hot poker. Darius sucking their marrow as if it were fine wine.

Yet, it didn't *feel* real.

Nor did the flashes of children flung into the night to defend themselves against the monsters alone.

He had the power to plant lies like seeds. To water those lies with the victim's doubt.

And still it was his head on the pike and not mine.

And terrible as those memories were, *I laughed*.

I had been that beaten child. Those monsters had already devoured me. It was my bones bashed into uneven brick and mortar in an unforgiving world that needed to feed.

It was a parlor trick of using my past, changing the hue, and pretending it was another.

I laughed harder.

Choking back a giggle once my mind flooded with images of a little boy who looked every bit mine—same features, same tenacity. But his blue eyes held none of my fear as he fought. His were the sea in a storm.

Refusal to submit.

And I knew as I saw him that no matter what the monster tried to show me, the little boy was real.

It was almost as if I could feel his little ghostly fingers curl around mine. The perfect greeting of a sweet child to a discombobulated stranger.

It was too real to bear.

"Mommy," the memory called out, as if we had known one another. There was the lie. Not the voice. No, that voice was very real. It was the word.

Mommy.

He did not know me. Just as Jade did not know me. Just as I had never known my mother.

"You will give me my son!"

"For a kiss."

No. Though the argument was personal, more had come to bear witness. The undead, hissing threats yet failing to come closer. As if there were an unseen line in the garden no toe might cross.

Lingering, circling, they called out obscenities. Clicked their tongues as if to draw my attention away. Others only cocked their heads as if this were the most entertaining display they had seen in ages.

More laughter.

But the unhinged sound was mine. I was laughing at *them*.

They were afraid of a head on a stick! The irony being that... so was I. I was petrified of a skull with sorry flesh hanging from its twitching muscles. One that could not touch me in any way that mattered.

One I was extremely tempted to simply... eat.

He was already inside my mind, why not just digest what was left? I could imagine the crunch of bone in a powerful maw. Even though the sound of those screams had been more beautiful than any the sun might inflict on the most terrible demon of hell.

Red eyes I remembered held mine as I said it. "I hate you."

I don't think I had ever said that to another being in my life.

But it was freeing! "I do, Darius. Not once did I love you. I might not remember, but I know I fought your desires."

And I had never fought Vladislov, not in that way. Not even on the planks when I'd let him have his show at my expense. No, I just ran, because I could not bear to look at him when he seemed so giddy.

And I would deal with him later.

What a thought. I would deal with the king of monsters, and I already knew he would kneel to me, perhaps even cry, but never learn.

In a very strange, comforting way, I could even accept that.

But first... Darius.

Lip curled, I stood just as I had seen my haughty daughter stand, snarling, "You'll be nothing but a display in a garden, scratching at the minds of those who wander too near in the same way mice scratch at the walls. You're a pathetic infestation, Darius."

"Kiss me, my treasure."

Oh, I'd kiss him all right. I'd eat his face right down to the bone!

Tongue already tracing the sharper edges of my teeth, I took a step closer, caught by a voice at my ear. "Pearl, this is no place for you."

What?

Who on earth would dare come between me and the finest, most pure moment of rage.

True hatred sang in me as if it had always been there, would always be there, and would give me all the comfort I lacked since my first breath.

What was love when hate might empower? What was love but a figment of the imagination?

Hate was far more real. It was palpable.

I could be whole!

A figure stepped into my periphery. "Look at me. One look and you'll understand why hate will never devour love no matter how hard it tries. Compassion triumphs over cruelty. Self-respect feeds while self-indulgence diminishes. Pearl. I'm right here."

A man, brown-skinned and beautiful in a way tranquil seas were beautiful. Eyes as hypnotic as waving barley in a soft breeze. Voice... his voice was water to quench an endless thirst. He offered a kind smile, even as he said, "This particular demon knows you in ways you cannot imagine. Look at your hands. Already, you're pulling Darius free of his prison. He's luring you into his whims, feeding your hatred."

What?

Oh God....

My outstretched hands *were* sticky with rotting ooze, both palms flush to the torn ribbons of throat that needed to be worked free. I had already pulled the snapping head a good three inches higher, fighting the crusting matter that had glued him in place.

I was touching the vilest of creatures, his crispy

skin cracking against my touch, his teeth bared as if once I pulled him to my bosom, he'd feast.

While I thought I was making a feast of him.

Desperate, the monstrosity screamed vileness into my mind as I yanked my touch away, and a sickening sound followed the head sinking down the pole until the tip hit the inside of his skull.

Its face was a frenzy of twitching, brains scrambling, healing, scrambling, healing. Just like me, there was a hole. A pike, taking parts away.

And in that, I took pleasure.

Even as I gagged.

The effort it took to break my gaze from the boiling crimson of a half-rotted head was almost unbearable.

As if it might make me clean, I scrubbed my hands on the silk of my skirt, the red growing grisly with the bits of unspeakable things. The stain on the outside matching the stain on the inside as that *thing* screamed for me to return.

Darius had been so close to freedom, in the arms of a daywalker who could move through space on an accidental whim. Who had fallen into his dream by teasing me with the angelic face of a dirty, suffering boy.

My boy.

Just like my girl, Jade.

"He has my son."

"He has nothing," the man said. "He's a head on a pike. One tormented knowing his heart beats in the chest of a good man."

Ignoring the ring of suddenly silent vampires—beautiful dead things that toed a line they could not cross—I faced the intruder.

And knew him.

Which was not comforting.

Arms folded under my breasts, further concealing my modesty from roving eyes, I saw the face he refused to offer on display at the wedding. And I found little gratitude considering all the years I called out for help and had been ignored.

"What do you think?" He was ignoring my narrowed eyes and heaving breath. "They fear their fallen king so much they cannot even step forward to snatch up two vulnerable daywalkers."

"You are not vulnerable." And he should not pretend as such.

Where brown eyes had dragged over the crowd, many vampires scampered back as though burned. They came back to rest on me. And gave me no pain.

Outstretching a hand, he said, "I'm not afraid of him."

"I am." That was not a hand I would take.

"I know. That's how darkness worms in. Evil

feeds on fear yet is slain by love." The answer was easy, even offered with a kind smile.

"And God is real. And the world should vibrate with forgiveness. And my children were taken from my body. And the only lover I've ever accepted used me as a prop to stage a show. And I am alone. And you hide your face." My lip shook, fresh tears falling as I struggled to say, "And your teachings were false."

"So much of what I tried to share was twisted, even by those who claimed to follow me. I said one thing, and they claimed another long after I walked away from the tomb. Believe me when I tell you that the truth is devoured. It has to claw its way out of the belly of the beast. It has to fight what it is being replaced with. And, in doing so, is altered." He looked pained. Endlessly sad. "I had been warned."

I knew. I had dreamed of those forty days and forty nights in the desert. "So what do we do?"

"I had been warned," he clarified. "But that didn't mean I was wrong to disagree. I still do. You have lived miracles. You have seen God work in such amazing ways."

Hysteric giggling preceded. "I have lived miracles?"

My faith was a joke. Jesus was insane.

Looking side to side as if taking in the artwork

of the landscape, the man said, "I have not been in this garden before. I imagine it must be quite beautiful in the sun."

Not that it was relevant, but it would be. There were fountains and flowers and little streams about, a façade to hide the ugliness of what lingered all over the grounds. "I didn't mean to come here."

"But here you came all the same. You cried out for home and slipped from one place to another. What does that say about you that *home* is at the feet of that thing?"

Ugly truth. I'd had enough ugliness for one night. "It says that I am—"

"Confused," Jesus, still holding out a hand to me, interceded. "Young. That's all you are. Please, I need you to take another step away from the demon."

"Why?"

"Because you are cutting into your wrist and you don't even feel the pain. All it would take is a few drops of you to worm his way deeper, and he possessed you long enough." His eyes pointed down to where my hanging fingers suddenly felt warm and icy all at once. "Don't you think?"

I was bleeding all over the grass, and not just a few drops. My nails had rounded into sharp little moonlight-white talons, and I had dug one in enough that bits of my torn muscle fibers were hanging from the corner of a claw. "Jesus!"

Tripping over my feet, that red dress, my panic, I put far more than a few steps between the head and my body—feeling a strain, almost to the point of a snap, between my mind and the mind of the monster who still played with me.

"This isn't funny!" No scream ever would be loud enough to trumpet that. Arm mending, my blood soaking into the dirt, and I was once again the laughing stock.

Those soft eyes turned toward the head, a frown turning a compassionate countenance into one of sadness. "But still, he laughs."

A grotesque cackle I could suddenly hear clear as a bell in my head. I could feel it on my skin. The papery dryness of a mummy possessing my body, and it tore my mind to shreds.

Hands to my ears, I screamed, "How can you stand it?"

"God is with me." It was then I noticed the threadbare cassock. A pauper's clothing, similar to what he wore as the old man at the wedding.

My dress was all the more garish beside it. "God has never been with me."

"Has he not? The tree branch that broke so you could be free of the noose? The snowfall after you'd been harmed by the lecher, a dust of pure white covering your tracks so you might find your way home to safety?"

I'd had enough of men of God, of the complete lunacy around me. "Then why was I hung by a priest? Why was I raped for walking home from work?"

It was as if I finally asked the right question. The man gave a breath of relief. "So that we could have this moment in a lovely garden, enjoying the view."

19

PEARL

Interlaced so tightly around in my grip that my fingers began to swell, the rosary grew red with my dripping blood. Cracked beads, a bent cross, the man depicted suffering upon it standing before me with his hand still outstretched.

A stranger to me, nothing like the vision I had clung to. As if he understood, as if he had witnessed this *revelation* more times than he could count, he crooked his fingers.

I filled them.

I filled that open palm with the lie of religion, abandoning my rosary and my blood-soaked utter stupidity in those waiting fingers.

Bead by bead, the string I used to say my prayers pooled in his palm. Red, damaged, but still beautiful. He let me look for as long as I could bear.

And then, as if reading his mind, he closed his palm and tucked the last vestment of my flagging faith away.

"How can you stand living with the lie?"

He didn't seem to mind that my blood smeared his hand and clothing. Offering an elbow as if to suggest we might take a stroll through nightmares, he said, "I tell everyone the truth. No one listens. So I speak as this man or that man. I speak as I always have. I call for compassion. But my father's world is so unbalanced. It only reflects what he's become. *There are the good parts.* There are the entertaining parts. There are the parts that love his son and his creations. And then there is the famished monster. Who eats, and eats, and kills. Who devours everything in his path all while searching for *you*."

The only thing I had anchoring me to this world, the one thing that had pulled me from the crypt, I knew was too good to be true and too ugly to be anything but beautiful in my eyes. "I'm not his wife or his soul. I can barely keep up with his chaos. I wasn't his sister or his queen in a past life. I was a waitress desperate to stay in the sun, who was afraid he would realize I needed him, that he did not need me, and that he will never really love me, considering what I am."

Gesturing toward the path, he led me away from the head and past the scattering undead, saying,

"Who are you to say what you are and what you are not?"

Excuse me? I was myself talking to a pretend demigod. Acknowledging that should have split me in half, but Darius had already done the rending. "I am *me*!"

That. That made Jesus smile. "A girl who dreamed of a window so she might sleep safely in the sun. A kind heart who wanted nothing more than to find a home."

"Your father can read my thoughts, you're doing the same. That does not mean you know me." Why were all these men so insufferable? Why was he leading me through a throng of hissing vampires who scurried away as if they might be burned by the very sunlight we discussed?

"I can't read your thoughts. What I know is because Vladislov has written to me of you. The detail in his letters… he is *deeply* in love. A phenomenon I never imagined I might witness, though he had told me stories of his lost wife."

My heart had been broken so many times. I had trusted adults. I had fought to please employers. I had wandered and begged God to lead me to someone, anyone who might take away what made me wrong. And where had God led me? To an alley where Malcom had ripped my fangs from my skull. But he had not been able to remove my cravings.

Where had God been in that? Where had God been while Darius had done things I could not recall? Lip shaking in a way I hated, eyes prickling, I dared to ask, "And all my prayers?"

Where my arm was tucked into his, he patted me gently. "God heard them."

No, he had not. And nor had this man. "But I prayed in your name. I prayed to your holy mother."

"And that was foolish. Where in the scant, centuries-old catalogued recordings of my teachings did I ever say that prayers should be made to me or to my mother? Would that not be idolatry?"

I had been raised on scripture. The words had been beaten into my back. "The New Testament—"

"Is a blend of megalomaniacs seeking worship and false prophets using my teachings to gain notoriety. Have you witnessed the vagaries of Twitter? It's the same phenomenon yet more pathetic. Weak souls driven to share their every vapid thought. Their sick fragility seeking validation. Cults flourish. So much filth is spread with the intent to do harm and gain a high in the process. No different than the men and women shouting as I bore my cross. You've seen it in your own life, felt the hurled stones hit your body. Everyone has their cross to bear. You have a tomb and a hole in your memories."

"And a daughter who despised the sight of me.

And a son you are trying to distract me from. Men think we don't know what you're doing. Women know. So stop wasting my time and tell me what Vlad had written of this boy in his letters." How much angrier should I be?

We turned at a cherry tree, following a path made misty from the damp lingering in the air. No undead approached. Instead, they still scattered as if there were a clear circle about us they were unable to traverse.

"Why aren't they hurting us?" A valid question, considering I could smell their intent on the breeze. Another valid question was why Vladislov had not come. Making me doubt him all the more. If he loved me, he would have come for me.

"Because I am not afraid of them," Jesus said, as if that explained everything.

The small pebbles lining the path under my feet squished when I dug in my heels. "I didn't mean to come here. Considering that all my life what I dreamed of most was to be in your presence, I'm finding now that I don't like you very much." Whatever he really was. "I want my boy, and I will leave."

My escort's footfalls ceased. "And when I tell you there is no son?"

"Then I'll call you a liar." My mind had been played with enough that I was beginning to see where the fingerprints led. In Darius' effective seduction, the boy he showed me *was real*. Alive now. *AND HE WAS MINE.*

Vladislov's son, a figure a huge portion of the world's population believed was their savior, said, "What you saw is feral, unnamed, and dangerous. It isn't a son, it's a burden."

Why mince words? "Because Darius made him that way!"

Jesus agreed, eyes full of pity, "Because Darius made him that way."

"You will give me my boy, or by God I will end you. You who I prayed to all my life and who could hear nothing because you are only a man." And men were fools who lied and tricked to get their way. "Your cassock doesn't change that."

"I'm glad you are beginning to recognize what you see. The cassock is only fabric with the intention to denote station. It's not real. I hung on a cross as long as you hung from a tree. My father, wings and all, rolled back the stone to set me free once he figured I'd learned a lesson. Stories came and grew wildly out of proportion, just as they will about you to Vampirekind, soul of Vladislov. You won't be able to stop it, though you will decry the tales time and again. You will be powerless over your own retelling. The wife of a God. The mother of a queen. The keeper of an untamed demon child."

His complaints or comparisons, I didn't care. I cared about his roundabout point. "You are not as different from your father as you might imagine. You're younger, prettier, but just as crazy."

His smile—I could see what was in that smile now. The smile of my fallen lord was full of secrets. "Your son will need a name."

"Jasper. That will be his name." Drawing my arm from the elbow of my companion, I faced him head-on. "Tell me what you want for him."

He took up the arm I yanked away, leading me toward a better-lighted path bursting with night blooming flowers and the scent of life. "Acknowledge that you are my father's wife, nothing more."

Torn red silk splattered with crusted guck, rotting matter, grass stains, and the acrid stink of fear-induced sweat. One tit hanging free. I was anything but a bride. "You want me to lie."

He shook his head, long hair waving in a way that was far too familiar. "I want you to admit what all of us who have seen you already know. My father isn't here, so grasp this moment in which I keep him away. The acknowledgment can be between us. Torment *him* for all eternity as he seeks out your favor. He deserves nothing less. But right here, in this garden, you and I will come to an understanding. Take him as your husband, and you'll save more than just the boy."

Fine. I'd trade the only currency I had if that boy would be laid in my arms. Vladislov could have my body and a troth. He would have taken both anyway. "He's my husband."

"Are you his soul?" The question was breathless.

"No." *Yes*.

Relief fell from the lips of a man I never wanted to see again—a man I wanted to get to know, whose knee I wanted to cry on—who was no different than his father.

And it seemed their agenda was not much different either. Though from where I stood, both of them were blind to that truth.

The family squabbles that would happen over the table would be interesting.

Jade and Malcom would watch them bicker, and I wondered if they would see it too.

Leaning forward to whisper atrocities in my ear, Jesus told me where my son was tucked away. Why he was there. How many I would have to kill to get him.

I didn't scream. Not then. What would the point be? I didn't rage at God for the unfairness of what had been done to a child. I simply nodded and turned away from *the son of God*.

And entered the Cathedral.

The path before me, it was as if I had walked it a

thousand times. Those who dared come near a mother seeking her child I killed with surprising ease.

And I drank.

And they ran screaming when the carnage in my wake was discovered.

Vladislov had made me strong. God had designed me to be deadly. Darius had wrung the goodness from me. And I had agreed to be wife to the Demon who controlled the world.

Glassy-eyed humans in pens, deep under the rot of the twisted church. Hundreds, thousands in the catacombs. They didn't speak at the sight of my blood-soaked body as I passed by. They didn't ask for help.

Their minds were mush, their state hardly above that of an animal.

Though I could have, I didn't help them. I wasn't there for them. I didn't even acknowledge them.

My mind was filled with the glowing beauty of a towheaded child that had his own pen, his own rags, his own snarling rage.

I tore the bars of his door right from the stone, bent metal… as if it were a simple task.

Scooping up a wild beast who tore into my throat in his hunger, I grew complete.

I sang as I rocked him, until the drowsy thing

had a full belly and I had a sleeping child in my arms. His head lolling against my shoulder, I carried him away from his suffering. I bore him out of the desecrated Cathedral straight out into the world.

My son.

He smelled of poison ivy, of birch, of blood, and of fire.

The sun rose as he indelicately snored. And he nuzzled against his mother, a stranger who wanted him.

Vladislov did find me in time, resting on a park bench, curled around my boy.

A boy he looked upon as if he saw through the pretty, filthy shell. Smiling, honest, Satan held out his arms to take the burden from me. I allowed it.

Cradling the still sleeping little one, he waltzed slowly around, humming a few bars. Our eyes met, my husband asking, "Can we keep him?"

Forever. "Yes."

"What bliss!"

20

VLADISLOV

The boy lying fast asleep upon the bed was an angel. Well, at least angelic in appearance. I couldn't even blame Pearl for falling in love with him at first *sight*.

Parted lips and apple cheeks smeared with dried blood, on an utterly cherubic face. He smelled of my wife, the same wife seated beside him as she continuously petted his matted, pale hair. I don't think the little thing had ever been bathed, not that I had any intention of poking around in his wee brain until greater topics had been sorted.

"Pearl, my darling, beloved wife, I'm angry with you."

Her hand stilled, just as filthy as the boy lying atop a pricy silk coverlet. It hovered, the tips of her claws unable to fully retract with her young near and a very real threat looming beside them.

"Don't think I can't see how you seethe, trying to hide it because the fate of the boy matters more to you than your pride. And I know why you're angry too. I can see that as well." Stooping down so my lips might brush her ear, I growled, "I can see right through you."

She didn't have an answer for that. How could she after the night she'd lived?

My Pearl may have refused the perfectly wonderful bath of blood I'd prepared with love, but she had bathed in plenty of blood on her own.

Drenched. I found her sitting in a human park in broad daylight looking like an extra from a horror flick. Rocking a small child in her arms, too taken with him to notice the looks she was garnering from the locals.

True to human form, no one approached what looked like a wild-eyed vagrant to offer help. Police were not summoned. Strangers walking dogs gave her a wide berth, their snapping little spaniels pulling at the leash to sniff at the bloody woman.

Anyone could have hunted and ended her, caught as she was in her distraction.

And they might have, considering the enemies she'd made in one night of bloodlust. Except I was watching over her. Giving her time to settle down and enjoy the feel of sunlight and the weight of her sleeping child in her arms.

"Running from me out of temper was unwise. I'd rather you strike me before—"

That was all the permission she needed, her upper body turning so she might lay open palm full-force upon my cheek.

I'm not sure who was more surprised. That even stung!

Where was I supposed to go with this? "Okay... that's a start."

"Don't you *ever* do that to me again!" Hackles raised, she stood from the bed, put herself physically between my body and the sleeping child as she railed. "You can't claim to love me and do something like that!"

My bride was too young to grasp that I did it *because* I loved her. "You could not have attended the wedding and failed to participate in the aftermath. It's expected to fuck in celebration, and rejection would have been a slight on the couple."

Arms crossed under her bosom, her free breast pushed up so invitingly it took all my will not to glance downward and lick my lips.

She hissed, "You could have warned me."

"You wouldn't have gone. And then you would have regretted missing what has thus far been the most important moment in Jade's life." Yes, I was highhanded. *I know that*. But I was also right.

My soul was in a state—an agitated, furious, angry state. The same tenor of state that had unraveled into a rather beautiful massacre. And yes, I had already heard *all about it*. It was all vampires could talk about, the story growing outlandishly garish.

The amount of complaints I had received. Yikes!

As if Pearl might have actually ripped a head from some old fart's shoulders. Please.

She didn't rip it off completely. She had delicately separated the majority of the throat, but her sweet little claws had not cut through the spinal cord. I'd seen the corpse as I had directed the cleanup.

Excellent work, I must say. Totally worth pissing her off, if that was the response I might get.

No one was going to fuck with my wife now.

Not when the vampire she had "dismembered" was so damn ancient he might as well have farted dust. The undead were terrified of the glowing angel.

I'd added in that last tidbit—glowing with sunlight that burned all who dared approach.

Dramatic stories were far more fun when they were peppered with a touch more flavor. I mean, how many times had a total stranger walked into a hive and just torn through the locals, draining them dry as if they were human cattle?

I heard all about how they had run screaming from the *avenging angel*. What a lark!

Considering a mass murder was not enough, the tale was far more outlandish. She had approached Darius and dared confront the maniac for his crimes.

A Daywalker reeking of my come.

As anyone who was actually important would have been at the wedding, who cared if Pearl had been a bit overzealous as she fed?

Her first real hunt!

What a success. And she got a prize.

A cute one that at first blush seemed perfectly innocent. At second glance just might be the antichrist incarnate.

"I have lived too long to see you risk yourself out of anger. And let's not pretend you won't be angry with me again. You were born angry. Just as I was born to rule you."

"No." Squaring her shoulders, Pearl unknowingly took on the mantle of a queen. Of my Goddess. "You were born to see in me a thing you want but will never completely have."

Oh no…

I was growing brave, and she could see it, and she was already growing angrier.

Pinching my pointed ear as if I were a child, she

dragged me from the room in which our little boy dreamed of rivers of blood.

And I let her.

She really had no idea the effect she had on me. If I just brushed the tip of my cock on her blood-soaked skirt, I was going to spurt.

Already, I was angling my hips, the urge ruined when she snarled, "Don't you dare."

But we were in our bedroom now. The bed was right there! And she looked absolutely delicious, and I wanted to fuck her, and *she admitted she was my wife*. "Please?"

That set her to screaming, Pearl threatening to leave me forever if I ever did something so horrible again.

I asked her to define horrible… and she struck me again.

Really hard!

Which made me really hard. Achingly hard.

My throbbing excitement leaked a string of pearly fluid that dangled from the tip, making her all the more enraged. So, I got down on my knees. "You can't be mad at me for seeing you like this and wanting to fuck you. You look glorious, my love!"

"I'm covered in dried blood *and other things*, in a torn, ugly dress, and I smell." Every word was shrill, Pearl tearing at her tangled hair in frustration.

"Exactly! *So pretty*! And please, darling, lower your voice before you wake up our son."

Those were not the right words, the woman on the verge of further violence. "He's *my* son. *Mine!*"

Ah, ah. I had been very careful with my word choice when I approached my angry woman in the park. "You said *we* could keep him. That makes him mine too. Also, you love me and want me to be happy. Don't try to deny it. You told Yeshua as much. Don't pretend you didn't. And don't gape at me like a fish when you know I can read the memory as if I was standing right there beside you." Palm to my heart, my entire being lit up in joy. "You even claimed to be my wife."

Her face was turning red, and not in embarrassment.

Holding up my hands, I softened my approach. "I know. He's tricky in the way he gets what he wants. He said you never had to *tell me*. He suggested that you could torment me by withholding the statement. And you will!" I smiled, the last vestments of my human mask fading and the real me on full display for her to enjoy. "You *will* torment me. But... you know just as well as he does that I can see all the beauty of your thoughts. So don't be mad at me or cross with him." My smile stretched, the hideousness of my mouth and all the sharp teeth on display. "Get it? Cross?"

"That is not...." But the corner of her mouth twitched.

Oh, but it was. "It is funny, my soul."

I was myself before her, all charred skin and crackling fire. Massive, winged, ugly, pure. Taking her dirty fingers, I brought them to my lips for a kiss. "I'm sorry. Really, I am. I have not felt fear in so long that when you disappeared last night...." What really was there to say? "I love you. I know you're angry. But you are only angry, truly angry, because you love me and it scares you."

Pearl worked to collect herself in her storm of feelings, letting out a deep breath as she snatched back her fingers and pressed her palms to her face. One moment passed, then another. Her breath slowed, her heart rate normalized. She peeked through her fingers and looked at me as if to say *what am I going to do with you?*

She was going to love me. Already, it throbbed in her chest right beside the annoyance. And it frightened her to no end.

But I reveled in both.

She was so stiff, and I was so much larger. So I let my wings hover around her slight form as if they might embrace her. "Pearl, do you want to talk about the Cathedral?"

"No."

"Should we discuss Darius?" She had withstood

far more than my son had given her credit for. That pussy was unable to know her like I did. Pearl *would* have eaten Darius' face down to the bone. Though I am glad she didn't. He probably tasted terrible.

Voice smaller, she answered, "I'd rather not."

It was like pulling teeth sometimes with this woman, but I loved every moment of it. "Okay. Then let me bridge the gap you have failed to address. Why haven't you asked me if I knew about the boy?"

Lips turning down in a frown, eyes flagging, my soul went from queen to grieving mother. "If you had known, you would have offered him to me in exchange for exactly what your son demanded."

She was so right. I which is why I had offered the boy when I really wanted to get my way and make her a bit less angry about the wedding thing. Though I had not anticipated Yeshua would act after only having seen my bride a single time. Though it would be a lie to deny I was grateful he had.

My worrisome boy wasn't usually so spontaneous. Which meant he was also desperate.

What Pearl really should really have been asking was, *how did my son know about the boy?*

God had not whispered that secret in his ear. I had. Tucked it right in his memories so the desperate

The Relic 223

bugger might have an opportunity to get what he wanted most.

For me to be laden with a soul.

And now I was. One who'd acknowledged she was my wife.

The part of me the fates had finally returned.

"Please tell me you love me, Pearl."

She wanted to say it badly, because she was infinitely good. She craved the moment she might divulge that there was more to her than confusion and sorrow. But she didn't have the conviction—

"I love you." Her voice had been small, her eyes on the floor when it slipped over her lips.

My jaw might have hit the floor. She admitted it! The wife I swept up and began waltzing around the room as my wings broke everything in their path said it.

And the pair of us were laughing.

This was *real*.

"I don't deserve you." I never would. EVER.

Laughing, she agreed, "You don't."

Swallowing her words, I kissed her so hard I knew my teeth tore at her lips. And I drank of my bride. I lapped at her closing wounds. I *ravaged*.

What I had done to her at the wedding had been calculating and boring. What I did to her then? Poets would write songs about it.

That dress, no matter how she gasped or bled at

my onslaught, was demolished. Her filthy skin, scoured clean by my tongue. In no way had she been ready to see the true starvation I endured or how it had to be quenched.

Had she not grown so fierce, she would have been terrified.

Each breast, those perfect, delicious tits, were worshiped. Wide, burning palms pressing them into her body, kneading the flesh, claw teasing the nipple so it might be sucked.

She screamed no. She screamed yes. She screamed for more.

She even screamed my name.

Right as I held up the monstrosity of my cock and lined it up where she was wet, aching, and owed. I told her I was going to fuck her for three days straight and offer no succor.

Not to my wife. Not to my queen. Not to the other half of me, the better half. The half that commanded such action by raising her hips and hissing when my hand went about her throat.

Milking my cock on that first thrust, she came.

She came, weeping with the joy of release.

And I fucked her.

No woman had ever been fucked the way my Pearl was fucked through those days, through those nights. Blood pouring from where I had slit my

The Relic

throat, I fed the monster who strangled my cock for more.

Deceitfully slight thing that she was, she worked to drain me dry in all ways.

I hurt her.

She hurt me.

I pleasured the Goddess.

She fed me the torment that made my sac draw tight.

That first time I came, the ground shook. The second time, bits of Paris began to crumble.

Soothing me with a soft touch, even as she rocked her hips over my exhausted form, Pearl asked me to leave the city in peace.

The words alone drew another bubbling of seed from my body, my thumb rolling her clit as I expanded almost to the point her pretty body might not take.

Weeping, she found another climax, sucking my offering deep.

And I knew, that was the one that would plant a baby that would grow in her womb.

A baby in which she would find joy.

EPILOGUE
VLADISLOV

"Why doesn't Mommy ever play with us?"

Because Mommy had been fucked senseless and was too tired to even feel when I carded my fingers through her hair. A pretty dark, waving lock I lifted off her pale cheek less than an hour before so sun might fall on her face as she slept.

Precious Pearl, always the napper, sleepy darling lass that she was.

"Mommy's body is busy growing your sister." Winking at the little hunter at my side, I said, "You've seen how big her belly is. She'd fall right over if she tried to run."

The kid laughed.

And adored me.

The feeling was mutual. So much so that my other son had shown up more than he was welcome, the jealous sot.

"I'm going to catch her something good to eat." And get all her kisses for it, no doubt.

Since she'd shorn him, washed him, taught him to speak, he was her world. *But I was her God.* Worshiped in the sun and in the moonlight.

Often, I had wept on her breast because the sensation of so true a love overtook me. I was her slave.

Which was why we now lived here, in the jungle, on an island where the world might let us enjoy what we were. Away from cities that quaked when my moods were free to roam. Away from Cathedrals she had a drive to purge.

And for sport, all the vampiric houses who wanted to survive my wife's reign dropped immortal treats into the jungle for our boy to snack on.

Down to his bones, that kid was a killer. Even I, the perfect predator, had not needed to teach Jasper how to stalk.

And Mommy didn't need to know that her occasional sip of morning blood had come from a screaming vampire her cute progeny had caught and dragged home especially for her.

He relished the screams, and he drained them

into a teacup. Because it had to be fresh for Mommy.

Silver platter and all, Jasper would carry it in with a smile. "Pretty Mommy, look what I brought."

Pretty Mommy would glow.

On her silk sheets. In the palace I ordered built for her. Where live-in staff treated my erection as a castle.

Yes, that was a penis joke.

There were *civilized* parties. There was passion. There was a garden tended by the only human on the grounds. One strictly off-limits to our son. Not that he had not tried a time or two.

Jasper was a real devil.

And Pearl knew it… and loved him anyway.

He brought her trinkets, sneaking out of his room while we slept. Amputated fingers, juicy leg bones… three times he tried to impress her with severed heads.

Which even I did not know how he found.

Because, once again, we lived on an island where there was none but us and those I knew were delivered.

Jasper, my beautiful, sweet, angelic boy, was a world ender.

One time, I cracked a joke that he was the antichrist.

Pearl refused to speak to me for almost a week.

She loved and she knew, fawning over her begotten monster as if the human jawbone he dug up that afternoon were a treasure.

I mean, *I made it a treasure* when I had it dipped in gold and set with diamonds.

I don't think a more elated boy might have existed in the world when he saw it. When he presented it to his mommy.

Who kissed him for it and playfully put it on her head like a crown.

Unlike our son, I knew she cried after I'd taken the kid for a stroll.

I knew she fretted.

I knew that was why Yeshua sat at our table and smirked at me at least once a month. That was why Pearl asked him to be her tutor so she might no longer be ignorant.

My son, *my obnoxious son*, agreed.

She bloomed under his tutelage.

She still didn't like him.

Who would? Her Jesus was a sanctimonious pain in the ass who refused to let a topic go, strangling the argument until there was nothing left but a carcass. He dumped way more dead things at my wife's feet than the boy she had taken from the pens.

The night Jesus dared offer her his wrist for dinner, I almost killed him. And that was not in the hypothetical sense.

He and I battled for a week, bouncing from landscape to landscape. We rent, we purged, we fought like the truly elemental things we were.

Until I heard my wife weeping from hundreds of thousands of miles away.

Hand around the throat of the *messiah*, I dropped him to the cracked dust and flapped my wings.

Jesus laughed, careless of the blood that dripped from his mouth. "You deserve everything that is coming to you."

Instantaneously, I found myself home, where women of my wife's acquaintance had gathered to cheer her out of the gloom that continued to upend civilization. Our son, Jasper, rested at her feet, his beautiful head on her knee—behaving himself in a way I had never witnessed.

Kicking free of his mother's embrace, he shot up... the babe stalking me as if I might serve as dinner. Fist in my face, he hissed. His first hiss. "Never leave her this way again."

His first hiss.

How could I not love this boy?

Eyes wet with unshed tears, Pearl looked up at me and welcomed me home. Proud as the queen she had grown to be.

What need had I of pride? Before the gathering of women there, I fell to my knees at her feet. Tired, focused, sorry. I prostrated where all those of rank in my presence would share the tale of the devil who loved an angel.

The angel who drank me down like wine after forgiveness was lavished on my form.

Dreaming of murder down the hall, Jasper smiled in his sleep. Diabolically entertaining, those dreams held my attention. I reveled in them.

Once, I even made the mistake of telling Pearl the best parts of our son's intentions.

The world would burn.

Terrified, she clung to me and begged that I might help him change.

Creatures didn't change, but I promised her I'd try.

That was the first night she felt our baby kick.

In one moment, her attention was on the vagrant. In the next, it was swallowed up by our baby.

Jasper was twice as enamored with what grew in Mommy's belly and fully in *love*.

Obsessed.

The ground shook, our *son* up to his normal tricks when he didn't get his way should she brush his incessant prodding off. He practically tore down our house when the fetus didn't respond to his songs.

"This is mine!" he would shout.

"She's not yours." Lips service I offered to

appease his mother. Because I knew just as Pearl feared that *he truly believed she was his*.

"Mommy, eat more. She's hungry." Jasper would rub that burgeoning belly. "Oh, and so pretty! We will be the best of friends. Her favorite color will be orange, and she will slurp down liver just like I do."

Jasper was not allowed to be present at the birth, the scamp unable to contain his excitement and far too distracting to the mother working to deliver. It was only the two of us while our son sulked in the jungle.

I was the first to see or touch our daughter, Pearl exhausted yet smiling when I set the babe on her breast.

Strength. Endurance. Intention.

The little girl was her mother incarnate.

As if he knew the moment his sister had taken her first breath, Jasper appeared and asked to hold her, the babe covered in vernix, mucus, and blood. His arms outstretched as if the only thing that might quench his endless appetite was soon to be delivered. Pearl made him wait, as the baby was learning to suckle.

The boy might have sacked an entire community in his temper, but his mother called him forward when his tantrum grew outlandish. She let him lay a single touch on her head.

A babe he longed would be his *best friend*.

And I knew what coursed through his veins. I had suffered the same.

Kissing my soul, I knew joy with my wife at the beauty of our child. Jasper named the babe—Beryl.

And dared call her his.

Pearl didn't tolerate it, chastising our son. "She isn't yours. She belongs to herself."

His soul, the mirror of mine, begged. "You're wrong, Mommy."

Our pretty phenomenon, Jasper... an amazing child. A true devil.

Who coveted, who hunted, and whom I found more than once standing over the cradle of my daughter, stroking her cheek and speaking of battles fought long before they were born.

Five times he threatened to kill me if I dared deny him his due.

So I did what had to be done.

I cast Jasper out to wander, removing all memory of him from Pearl's mind so she might enjoy her daughter without the constant worry over her son—a deadly son who had been born to run wild and was growing all the more manic caged by an island too small to satiate his whims.

I told him this, honest when I dropped him at the doorstep of the Cathedral.

He might have only been a boy, but he had the

memories of a man. Until he grew into his body and learned to control his urges, he was not to be permitted near his mother or his sister.

After all, eternity was a long time. What might a few dozen years mean in the scheme of things?

Jasper didn't wail. He didn't cling to me. Instead, he made an oath.

To bring the world down in flames if his soul was not returned to him. Tussling his hair, I was so proud, knowing exactly how he felt, and glad I hadn't had my Pearl in those hungry centuries where I wreaked havoc.

The kid would do well getting it out of his system. Then he might return to the flock, where he would find it was not his sister he was drawn to. It was the possibility for what might have been in her. Whoever he had lost and been reborn to find would not be delivered so easily.

He'd have to search for her. Suffer for her. Learn to control himself so as not to frighten her with his greatness.

And when he saw her, he'd know.

There was no need for him to project what he saw in Mommy and Daddy.

He'd know.

The boy nodded, threw a rude gesture my way, and told me he would get even with me for this, before turning his back and climbing the steps of his new home.

I believed him.

That would be fun!

"I'll come visit tomorrow! Be a good boy!"

Heaven help the woman he fell in love with.

Chuckling, I returned to my wife, smiling to find her in such peace. Babe in arms, she danced around our room, humming in the sunshine, all the constant niggling worry over her beautiful boy lifted away.

An indulgent smile paired with beautifully sparkling blue eyes. "Welcome home."

Kissing the top of Pearl's head, I brushed the back of a claw down the smiling cheek of my sweet little girl. And all was right in the world.

Thank you for reading THE RELIC? Craving More? Please enjoy an extended excerpt of SWALLOW IT DOWN...

SWALLOW IT DOWN

Dripping, swampy sweat had gathered between Eugenia's breasts. Her mouth a desert. Knowing exactly how foul the act was, she delved dirty fingers between slimy mounds to bring the salty brine to parched lips.

And she sucked them clean, ignoring the taste of road dust.

Scrambling to cover exposed skin, cleavage was concealed. From head to toes, her body fully draped to protect from the relentless sun. That same protection half the reason she was melting alive in no man's land.

Sweat. Or burn and sweat. A lose-lose situation.

Wide-brimmed hat, woven by hand and ugly as the day was long, kept the sun off her face. A bandana kept the dust out of her mouth. Layers of repurposed tee-shirts, badly sewn together animal skins, jeans, sneakers on the verge of losing their soles. Torn bits and bobs, a sea of safety pins and animal gut thread keeping her just as fashionably disgusting as everyone else since the world ended.

And the goddamn sun was relentless, miles yet

until she might reach where Fresh Water marked her map.

It had been two days.

Two days without fluids was enough to kill in this kind of heat.

A lapping lakeshore—spanned by the raggedy stone bridge underfoot—was just another reminder that nothing could be trusted. Murky, undrinkable water taunted travelers. Water that had tempted many to take a sip. Eugenia had seen enough corpses on the road not to fall for nature's trick.

Not to listen to the sweet splashes as she pined for a drink.

It had once been so easy to grab a bottle of chilled water from the fridge. To not question the source or the safety. Food had been abundant and full of variety. People used words like *organic, vegan, prime*...

Now? Not so much. Eat what you find or don't eat at all. And that included the rare expired snack food that one would think might be exciting when the menu often included grubs, but really... the taste of *before* didn't come with a sense of nostalgia. It came with a knife of remembrance.

The stone bridge. The water. The dead forest taunted her enough with what the world had been. A rare find of Cheetos just pissed her off.

Humid air rustled through branches, but there

was no whisper of leaves sighing as trees swayed. Only the bony noise of clicking, snapping wood.

Pathetic last words, but worth muttering. "What I wouldn't give for air conditioning."

The man plodding on at her side grumbled, "They got that up in city. If you'd just go to one, you can pay for cool air like everyone else."

John wasn't the worst companion she'd met on the road. Of a similar age, strong enough to carry his own pack and contribute, he was the quiet sort. Only got handsy with her once. Learned his lesson and remembered the manners his mother must have taught him before nuclear war fucked up everything everywhere.

"Need I remind you, John, this *shortcut* was your idea." He'd strongly suggested this very route, leaning over her without so much as brushing her shoulder when they came to a crossroads and she had to decide left or right.

With a slanted grin, he shrugged. "According to your map, this trail took two days off the journey to Fresh Water."

It wasn't a trail if the road was paved, but there was really no point in correcting him. Especially since she had agreed. The reason she'd agreed? Because it also kept them farther from the marked settlements on her map.

Even better, travelers avoided the dead woods

The Relic

under the false assumption that the forest was toxic. But there were no char marks or wilting. None of the telltale signs that hinted at radiation. The trees were dead, true, but they were also decaying. Irradiated woods didn't decay, because they lacked the microbes responsible for recycling organic matter. These trees died after the bombs fell.

Gypsy Moths.

The forest died when, year after year, caterpillars decimated their leaves—damaging the tree's ability to respirate and gather energy from the sun. Trunks fell and rotted like they were supposed to. Many lay in the road, slowly turning to sawdust.

There were bugs to eat. There were animals to hunt. There were other things growing like weeds on a grave, which meant there was also rain.

Not that Eugenia had enjoyed a sudden thunderstorm or the relief of water she might actually drink falling from the sky. From the look of the dried-out body face down in the middle of the bridge, that poor soul hadn't felt the rain either.

Rushing to pillage the corpse's pack, John pulled the zipper and found... nothing of value. Eugenia could have told him that. If the person had water, they wouldn't have died on the middle of a bridge, face down and mostly ignored by the wildlife.

Let the man moan and curse.

John's frustration was hers; it was everyone's in

the dead world where nothing was easy and everything hurt.

A world greedy humans ruined.

A spoiled world in which Eugenia had been crushing her second year of med school. Harvard, full scholarship.

Then the bombs fell; cities were wiped away in a blink. She'd been camping with friends. Friends who were all dead now, or being whored. Or died being whored. She didn't know.

Couldn't think about it too hard. Just like she wouldn't think about who the corpse might have been.

Because whatever existed before was gone.

The dark ages were back with a vengeance, and *City*. City was a cesspool. Didn't matter which one. No sanitation, roving gangs always fighting for territory, the only way most women might make a buck was on their backs.

And considering the extreme increase in violence against women once the world went to hell, there weren't all that many women left.

So fuck City. And considering the types she'd kept up with since the fall, fuck men in general.

John wasn't so bad. But if he looked at her with that puppy stare one more time, she just might pop him in the mouth.

Leaning against a crumbling stone side rail, she

watched John pick through the corpse's pockets, wondering when someone would be doing that to her. And boy would they be disappointed. She had nothing others would find valuable in her pack—the pack itself faded from the blue it had been when new. Torn here and there. Empty of supplies. Heavy, because no matter how bad things got, both volumes of *Nelson's Textbook of Pediatrics* went where she went.

He flipped the corpse over to rifle through what rotting tatters might conceal, the body seeming to smile up at her.

Eugenia didn't smile back.

"We need to get moving." Or this was how she was going to die.

On an endless stone bridge in dangerous, unknown territory, seeking water that was so close she could taste it. Going mad from the sound of tainted drink just a few feet away.

No different than the other bodies they'd found on the road. The whole bodies, the bloated bodies, the dried bodies, and... well... the bits of bodies left after wild dogs found supper.

Man's best friend wasn't so friendly once it started starving.

Which was a pity. Eugenia had grown up with such a great mutt. She still liked dogs. And they liked her too... for a snack.

Killing that first pup in self-defense had been harder than knifing a man trying to get into her pants.

And they all tried.

Which was precisely why she'd been forced to leave her former accommodation, again, and make her way south to new territory.

Where she'd picked up John wallowing on the side of the road. Where she didn't make small talk but shared her supplies.

Everyone held on to something from the past.

John's seemed to be a sense of optimistic stupidity.

Eugenia's was sheer stubbornness and an undying sense of anger that—thanks to a shit president and a fucked-up world—all her dreams had been blown to ash. All her hard work, all the sacrifices she had made to achieve her goals… useless.

Two years of med school did not make one a doctor. A medic, in theory. Which had been handy when there was nothing to trade. But a medic with tits wasn't safe.

She learned that lesson in the first disease-riddled settlement. AKA, the shanty town of Wellspring.

Pretty name for an awful place.

And in the years since, there wasn't any place she wandered by that wasn't awful. Might as well pick one and plant her flag. Give up on her life as a vagrant. Live where sewage collected on the streets and everyone was sick from dirty water and improper hygiene. Try to make things better.

But, if they didn't get moving, she was going to die on that long, stone bridge, never knowing air conditioning again. John would probably take her stuff and die a mile or two up the path. Another traveler would loot his corpse. Just as she had looted bodies for years and pretended not to cry.

There wasn't any moisture for tears now. No point in regrets. But still, that kernel of anger festered, because her perfect future had been stolen by power-mongering boneheads. And six years of living a hard life had not broken her as quickly as it had the others.

Which was unfair.

Why care anymore? Why keep looking for a good place and good people?

"Do you see that?" John, wasting precious energy, waved his arm toward a portion of the lake obscured by dead trees.

"Yup, it's water."

"I didn't think the stories were real, but I'll be damned. They even got power!"

Electricity was only in City, and even there it was hard to come by, spotty, and cost more than just a cock in the cunt. Anal. That's what it cost.

Yet, a glitter broke through the copse of decaying trees. Electric light. Which meant water.

Which meant survival.

Already making a mental list of the crap in her pack, trying to scrounge up any idea of what to trade for a full canteen. Shamefully daydreaming of air conditioning and a soft bed.

Knowing full well that an ocean liner had no business in a freshwater lake. That electricity didn't exist in the no man's land on her map. And that she'd gone too long without hydration and was hallucinating.

"Wait." The word was dry, so dry that even though she tried to stop him, John had already begun to run toward the shore. Splashing through sludge, having left his valuables right there on the shore, he dove in, swimming toward the enormous, shining boat.

Something wasn't right.

Who uses electricity when the sun is up? That awful gut feeling that kept her as safe as one might be in this new world clenched so hard it stole her breath. This wasn't a good place. This wasn't a good place if no one knew about it and no map she'd seen marked a moored, massive ship large enough to hold thousands.

But there were people on the landing, coming out at John's hollering. There was a red-carpeted gangplank leading up to the upper levels, welcoming passengers as if they were about to take Eugenia's dreamed-of cruise to the Bahamas.

There would be water. Filtration systems that pumped out water she could actually drink.

"John, come back!" But he ignored her, swimming on.

And she could see those few gathered outside were armed. Men pointing right at her as if to say, *"Collect that."*

Because *this was a bad place*.

And thanks to John, they had seen her.

Options were limited. Swim across the lake and face whatever might be found on her terms. Or, wait for the party already boarding a dinghy to come chase her down in the woods.

She didn't have the strength to run. She didn't have the strength to swim.

But no way on God's dead earth was she going to stand on the shore and be collected.

Potentially drowning in that lake would be better than dying under strangers, chased down by the men earnestly slicing oars through water to reach her.

Men who didn't call out a greeting. Men who looked large and well fed.

And don't forget those guns. Big ones.

Considering it was so fucking hot, why not take a final swim?

Let them see she was not afraid. That she never buckled. That she was smarter than leading them on a merry chase through dead woods.

And that was that.

Off went the hat, the backpack with her precious volumes, the outer layers that would come between her filthy skin and cool, murky water. In she went, swimming for the ship. Knowing she'd never make it.

But she did.

The human condition wouldn't let her sink. Delirious, the body fought the mind and she cut through the water like a fish. Fingers reached the bobbing gangplank, having somehow passed the boat, somehow passed John, who splashed in her wake.

A stranger's firm hands pulled her from the lake, where she fell immediately to her back, staring up at a sun so blinding she couldn't make out the shadowed faces standing over her.

"Well, aren't you a pretty one?" Someone was pawing at her face, turning her chin and brushing wet, red curls off her cheek.

Trying to swat off the attention was almost more effort than her exhausted muscles might put forth. "Hands off the goods."

"And bossy to boot."

The sounds of her companion being pulled from

the water, of his sputtering and coughing, were ignored. Eugenia, still blinded by the sun but doing her damnedest to point her eyes in the direction of the dark figure hovering closest, muttered, "Mister, just tell me one thing. You got air conditioning on this ship?"

A masculine chuckle was the only answer supplied.

Her companion coughed, then sucked in a breath to say, "Brought the girl for sale. As you can see, she's a beauty. A great ride too."

John. Fucking puppy-eyed John.

How dare he! After she'd hunted for him, shared resources... allowed him to travel with her and glimpse the precious map.

Even though someone held a canteen to her lips, even when clean water warmed by the sun splashed her tongue and was gulped. Right then, right when that water hit her gut, she knew it. John had been planning to sell her all along. That's why the pussy kept pushing for City. That's why he suggested the *shortcut* when his whining never won her.

His voice was coming closer. John crawled near where she guzzled. "Do we have a deal for the girl?"

"No." Authoritative, definite.

Maybe there was a God.

Or maybe there was just nothing but evil. "A slave can't sell a slave. You want water, boy. You work for it. If you don't work, you get tossed over with the rest who failed to pull their weight."

In raggedy underclothes, head pounding, muscles noodley, Eugenia found the strength to lean up on an elbow and spit every drop of life-saving water in her mouth at the traitor. "Pig!"

The same man who had deemed her a slave at first glance ordered, "Get her off the ramp before that creamy skin burns. Take her to the women on Level 15—*in the air conditioning*. Have them clean her up and keep her alive. This siren's too valuable to let die."

Fighting with the little strength she had, biting, hoarse screams, and pathetic flopping did nothing to keep her from being shouldered like a knapsack.

It wasn't a short walk, but she didn't give up, powerless to move her arms more than a sorry swing but sharp with her tongue. She threatened the stranger's life, swore she'd tear off his cock if he put it anywhere near her. His mother. His family. Creative in her expletives until a door opened and cool air blasted her back.

There really was air conditioning on that boat! One taste of it on her skin and she went from spitting hellcat to sobbing wreck.

The trivial thing she'd craved most from the life stolen when the bombs fell was just as divine as she remembered.

"Hey, Joan, here's a new one. Captain wants her cleaned up and kept alive. Level 15."

"Well"—a woman spoke, a no-nonsense, middle-aged voice—"won't that just get the men frothing at the mouth? And just look at all that red hair."

"Temper to match. She's a biter." Hefting Eugenia down against something soft and forgotten, the bruiser who dragged her into air-conditioned hell warned Joan, "Watch yourself."

"Yeah, I heard you. Now go. No men are allowed up here until the bell."

Ready for more?

Read SWALLOW IT DOWN now!

ADDISON CAIN

USA TODAY bestselling author and Amazon Top 25 bestselling author, Addison Cain's dark romance and smoldering paranormal suspense will leave you breathless.
Obsessed antiheroes, heroines who stand fierce, heart-wrenching forbidden love, and a hint of violence in a kiss awaits.

For the most current list of exciting titles by Addison Cain, please visit her website: addisoncain.com

facebook.com/AddisonlCain
bookbub.com/authors/addison-cain
goodreads.com/AddisonCain

ALSO BY ADDISON CAIN

Don't miss these exciting titles by Addison Cain!

Standalone:

Swallow it Down

Strangeways

The Golden Line

The Alpha's Claim Series:

Born to be Bound

Born To Be Broken

Reborn

Stolen

Corrupted

Wren's Song Series:

Branded

Silenced

The Irdesi Empire Series:

Sigil

Sovereign

Que (coming soon)

Cradle of Darkness Series:

Catacombs

Cathedral

The Relic

A Trick of the Light Duet:

A Taste of Shine

A Shot in the Dark

Historical Romance:

Dark Side of the Sun

Horror:

The White Queen

Immaculate

CPSIA information can be obtained
at www.ICGtesting.com
Printed in the USA
LVHW090040180222
711446LV00015B/100

9 781950 711604